Chosen Mate

Catamount Lion Shifters, Book 2

By J. H. Croix

This is a work of fiction. Names, characters, businesses, places, events and incidents are either the products of the author's imagination or used in a fictitious manner. Any resemblance to actual persons, living or dead, or actual events is purely coincidental.

ISBN: 1530006422
ISBN 13: 9781530006427

Dedication

To my favorite girls.

Sign up for my newsletter for information on new releases!

http://jhcroix.com/page4/

Follow me!

jhcroix@jhcroix.com
https://twitter.com/JHCroix
https://www.facebook.com/jhcroix

Centuries ago in the northern Appalachian Mountains, mountain lions fled deeper and deeper into the mountains, seeking safety from the rapid encroachment of humanity into their vast territory. Mountain lions developed the power to shift from human to mountain lion and back again, saving their species as they hid in plain sight. The majestic wild cats became creatures of myth. Reported sightings were treated as wildly speculative rumors. Impossible. Until one evening on a busy highway, a car struck an animal in the dark. The first confirmed sighting of a mountain lion in the East in close to seventy-five years. The wild cat was dead, its unbelievable existence snuffed out by a car. This mountain lion wasn't just any mountain lion. Though its autopsy would only reveal it was, in fact, a mountain lion and that the lion had improbably traveled over 1,500 miles from South Dakota, the longest known journey for such a creature. In Catamount, Maine, shifters lived amongst the world, having successfully protected their very existence for centuries. Until one of their own died an improbable death, and they learned of a threat facing their kind.

Chapter 1

Jake North woke with a jump when the door to his office opened. "Huh?" he said groggily.

"Seriously, Jake? Did you sleep here last night?"

Jake rubbed his eyes and ran a hand through his hair, looking up to find Phoebe Devine standing beside his desk.

"I guess so," he said. He sat up straighter and rolled his neck from one side to the other, a weak effort at easing the tension from sleeping in his desk chair. Glancing at his computer, he saw it was still on. Multiple screens were loaded with the searches he'd been working on last night.

Phoebe smiled softly and handed him a cup of coffee in the distinctive bright blue takeout cups from Roxanne's Country Store. He gratefully took it, immediately taking a swallow, the rich flavor welcome.

"Thank you," he said. "To what do I owe this morning gift?"

Phoebe plopped down in the chair on the opposite side of his desk. "I thought I'd check in since your car is covered in about a foot of snow. I figured you'd stayed late and fallen asleep." She paused, her dark brown eyes concerned. "You've been working so hard on this investigation since Callen died. I know how important it is, but I'm worried about you. It wouldn't hurt to take a break every so often," she said softly.

Jake took another sip of coffee and looked across his desk at Phoebe. She was a good friend. One of the few friends he could trust in the aftermath of the bombshell that had dropped in Catamount, Maine, a community along the vein of Maine forest through which the Appalachian Trail traversed. Just over a month ago, a mountain lion had been killed on a highway in Connecticut. Turned out, the mountain lion in question was a shifter from Catamount – Callen, a shifter from an old family of shifters. Jake's family was as old and storied as Callen's. Both were founding families of Catamount, one of the oldest and most well-protected shifter strongholds in the East.

As if Callen's death weren't devastating enough, Jake had started sleuthing in Callen's email accounts at the request of Callen's brother-in-law, Dane, who also happened to be Jake's closest friend. Jake's expertise was computers, specifically writing code and hacking. Most of his hacking was above-board, but when needed, he could chase down almost anything. In this case, he wasn't so sure if that was a good thing or not. Though he still didn't know why Callen died on that highway, he knew Callen had been coordinating for Catamount shifters to be used for drug smuggling activities by someone out West. That nugget of knowledge had exploded into public view after Dane's new fiancée, Chloe, had been kidnapped to use as leverage last week. Chloe was safe and sound now, but no one knew who to trust because it was clear Callen hadn't been working alone.

While the shifter community had been reeling from

Callen's death, they now had to grapple with an overwhelming sense of betrayal and fear. In the secretive world of shifters, trust was hard enough to come by. With shifter safety and existence at stake, Jake had been working relentlessly the last few weeks. Centuries of protection were at risk due to Callen's betrayal. Jake looked at Phoebe, taking in her dark eyes and long dark curls. Concern shone in her expression. He sighed. "I know, I know. I should take a break, but we have to get to the bottom of this. After what happened to Chloe…"

"Stop it," Phoebe ordered, cutting him off. "We all know Catamount shifters are in danger right now, but a few hours of sleep isn't going to change that. Plus, you're not much good to anyone if you can hardly keep your eyes open."

Jake grinned. "True. Well since I missed a good night's sleep last night, will you take my word for it that I promise I'll leave the office tonight by seven and go home?"

Phoebe shook her head. "Nope. I'll meet you here and make sure you leave. You're having dinner at my place tonight. After you have a decent meal, then I'll make sure you go home."

He chuckled. "You don't even trust me to go home afterwards?"

Phoebe smiled broadly. "Definitely not. I know you. You'll talk yourself into driving back to the office because you'll feel better after a decent meal. You need sleep, and I've decided to make sure you're going to get it. That's what friends are for," she said firmly.

Relief and appreciation washed through him. He'd been pushing himself so hard, he couldn't remember the last time he'd had a decent meal. He'd even skipped Thanksgiving dinner yesterday because he'd been deep in the files of one of Callen's contacts out in Montana.

"Is Shana still staying with you?" he asked.

Shana was Dane's younger sister, Callen's widow, and Phoebe's best friend. She was completely devastated to learn about what Callen had been planning. Shana was a shifter as well, also from a founding family in Catamount. She was struggling to adjust to the knowledge that the man she loved had put the entire shifter community in Catamount at risk by revealing who, what, and where they were. Even worse, he'd planned to make money off of them. Shana had been staying with Phoebe since they discovered what happened to Callen.

Phoebe shook her head. "She said she felt like she had to face what happened. She moved into the old guesthouse on Dane's property. She's been over almost every day, but she's not staying with me anymore."

Jake nodded. After another swallow of coffee, he stood and stretched. "How about I take you to breakfast?"

"Only if you promise to meet me for dinner tonight and go home afterwards."

Jake couldn't help but smile. Phoebe was nothing if not protective of her friends. "I promise," he said firmly.

***

Phoebe absently ran her finger around the rim of her wineglass. "Well do you think the Fish & Wildlife guy in Montana is bad news or not?"

Jake arched a brow. "The problem is my gut tells me he's a good guy, but the computer trail isn't pretty. He was a main point of contact for Callen out there."

"So why do you think he's a good guy?"

Jake shrugged. "No good reason." He couldn't put his finger on it, but the man in question seemed to have discouraged Callen from something he was planning. The details were vague, but Jake just didn't get the sense the guy was in cahoots with Callen.

Phoebe pursed her lips. "Well, you can't trust him then."

Jake chuckled. "The list of people I trust is very short right now. I won't be adding anyone without extensive checking first. Aside from you, my parents, my sister, Dane, Shana, and Roxanne are about the only people on it."

Phoebe sighed and brushed her hair out of her face. True to his word, Jake had met her at his office and come to her place for dinner. He hadn't put up an argument when she insisted he ride with her. She looked across the table at him, and her heart clenched with worry. Jake was one of her best friends. She'd had a terrible crush on him in high school, what with his golden brown hair, bright blue eyes, sculpted face, and a hard body to die for. Phoebe hadn't dared let herself think he could ever be anything other than a friend. She wasn't a shifter, and Jake came from one of the oldest shifter families in town. Phoebe had cousins who were shifters, which is how her parents ended up Catamount, but she wasn't. So she'd taken her high school crush and tucked it away in a corner while Jake had become one of her closest friends.

In the shadowed light from the candles and the light over the stove, the feline cast to his features was more pronounced. His deep blue eyes tilted at the corners, his sensual mouth quirked when she stood to pick up their plates.

"I can get those," he said, starting to get up.

She put a hand on his shoulder. "Sit."

He chuckled. "It won't kill me to carry my plate to the dishwasher."

Phoebe opened the dishwasher and quickly put the

dishes inside. When she turned back around, she found Jake right behind her. “Oh! I didn’t hear you.” She tried to check her pulse, but it raced ahead. He was too close for comfort.

His mouth quirked as he held up her wineglass. She took it from him. “I wasn’t done yet.”

He didn’t reply and leaned against the counter. He was physically commanding in the small kitchen. He eyed her. “I kept my promise.”

She wasn’t sure what was happening with her, but Jake like this was crossing her signals and making her body run wild. After years and years of training herself to remember he could never be anything but a friend and keeping her body under strict control around him, it was as if she’d forgotten the hopelessness of letting herself want him. And oh, did she ever want him. Right now, in the dim, shadowy kitchen, heat coiled inside her belly and suffused her body. The claws of desire pricked her skin. Her heart beat wildly, her face flushed.

She looked up at Jake, praying her expression was composed. “You did. But you’re not done yet.”

His blue eyes held hers. If she hadn’t known better, she’d have thought she saw desire darken them. But that was impossible, so she didn’t even entertain the thought.

“I’m not?”

She shook her head, desperately trying to keep her wits while her pulse pounded and her body felt as if it were being pulled to him by a magnetic force. “You have to go home and sleep. No working tonight. That was the promise.” She was breathless and barely managed to keep her voice level.

You have got to stop this. Jake is off limits. You’ve had it under control. Don’t lose it now.

Phoebe felt frantic inside. She needed to get her

wits about her. Jake pushed away from the counter and took one stride, which brought him just in front of her. The heat of his body tugged at hers. She tried to calm her heart rate, but her body ignored her mind. *You're freaking out because of this awful mess. You're just scared. That's what it is. After what happened to Chloe, you're scared for everyone in town, especially shifters. Jake could have been hurt when he helped Dane rescue Chloe. That's all this is. Your emotions are running wild.*

Upon the heels of this reasoning, Phoebe made the stupid assumption that the heat would stop swirling inside of her, her pulse would slow down, and she'd be able to look at Jake without melting. When she looked up into his dark blue eyes, molten heat built inside. The desire she'd somehow kept in check for years ran rampant through her body. Her heart pounded so hard, she feared he'd hear it.

She bit her lip and closed her eyes. They flew open when she heard Jake swear softly. The moment her eyes opened, his lips landed on hers. She was lost. He kissed her fiercely, sweeping his tongue inside her mouth when she gasped. She might as well have gone up in flames right then and there. Years and years of denial lent a depth of power to Jake's touch. His kiss nearly brought her to her knees. One of his strong arms swept around her, sliding down her back in a heated caress and cupping her bottom to tug her against him. The hard, heated evidence of his arousal pressed into the cradle of her hips.

Wet heat built inside of her, drenching her with desire. Jake simply kept kissing her—hot, deep, open-mouthed kisses. Their tongues tangled. She gasped for air when he tore his mouth from hers, blazing a path down her neck. Her name fell from his lips in a soft chant between nips and kisses. He swiftly unbuttoned her blouse, pausing for a long moment when he came to the black lace of her bra. Her nipples strained against the lace, tight and achy with want.

She could barely breathe, but she had to make this stop. It couldn't go further, or she wouldn't be able to face it when Jake realized this was a mistake, an aberration.

"Jake," she whispered furiously. "We have to stop."

His eyes were pinned to her breasts. Phoebe tried to step back, but the counter was behind her. She reached between them and tugged her blouse together, ignoring the desperate call of her body.

"Jake." She repeated his name, flinching at the hint of sadness in her voice.

He lifted his eyes to meet hers.

***

Jake stared at Phoebe, scrambling to gain purchase in his mind. She felt so good, so damn good. He'd wanted her for so long and was weary of denying himself. Yet, he couldn't have guessed at how phenomenal it would feel to touch her, to kiss her, to feel her flex under his touch, come alive in his arms. The cat in him stirred, the depth of his primal desire a living, breathing force he could barely keep leashed.

Phoebe said his name again, her voice tinged with the barest hint of sadness. He wanted to pull her close and tell her not to worry, there was nothing to be sad about. *This* force between them was about the only right and true thing in his life. But he'd denied his desire for her for so many years for good reason. When they were younger, he hadn't wanted to take advantage. That was only one reason for steering clear of her. He'd been raised a shifter among humans. Shifters had survived as they had by blending in. His family told tales of generations of shifters scrambling to survive until their numbers were enough that they could breathe easier. Though it had never been explicitly stated, Jake had grown up assuming he'd fall in love with another shifter. Then he'd stupidly fallen in lust with Naomi in college and realized what an utter disaster it could be for shifters to fall in love with humans. One stupid college relationship had led to far too many disastrous rumors. He'd sworn off even considering a relationship with any woman who wasn't a shifter. *But Phoebe's different. You know she's different.*

He could hardly bring himself to stop staring at her. He'd fantasized about her for years. Her generous breasts strained against the black lace of her bra, her nipples taut. Hints of pink peeked at him through the lace. He flicked his eyes to hers and saw the answering desire in hers. He knew, he'd known for years, that she wanted him as much as he wanted her. They'd done this dance of friends for so long, they were experts at it. But now, now that he'd had a taste of her, he couldn't stop. Not just yet.

Holding her gaze, he slipped his thumb under the clasp between her breasts. With a snap, the lace fell open, her breasts exposed to him. She gasped, her dark eyes wide. His eyes fell, his pulse pounding in his ears. Her breasts were round and full, the nipples dusky pink. Instinct drove him. He brought his hands up to curl around them, rubbing his thumbs over her peaked nipples. Her breath came in ragged gasps. He finally gave in and leaned forward to tug a nipple into his mouth, her sharp cry bringing his cat to quietly growl under the surface of his skin.

By the time he pulled away, both nipples were damp, glistening in the soft light in the kitchen. He was pulled tight with the depth of his want for her. He brought his eyes to hers again.

"Jake," she whispered. "We have to stop."

For once, he didn't want to listen to the bitter side

of himself, the side that had told him for years he could never consider loving a woman who wasn't a shifter. Because they couldn't understand, they might betray him and his kind. With Phoebe, he knew that wasn't true. He trusted her completely.

He shook his head slowly. "But we don't. I know you want this as much as I do," he said softly.

Phoebe stood in front of him, her breasts rising and falling with her ragged breath. Her dark hair tumbled in loose curls around her shoulders. Confusion and sadness flashed through her eyes. "I don't understand what's happening," she said.

"We're finally doing what we've both wanted to do for years." He stroked his hands down her shoulders and along her arms, his hands coming to rest at the juncture of her elbows. He wanted her with a depth beyond reason, but he knew if he didn't allow it to happen when she felt ready, it could devastate their friendship and ruin any chance for him to have what he'd denied himself for so long. A tiny, bitter corner of his mind pointed out that he was breaking his own rules here and he'd likely live to regret it.

"You've wanted to do this for years?" Phoebe asked.

Jake's heart clenched. He hid his feelings so well she didn't even know. He nodded slowly. "Yes."

She stared at him, her eyes skating over his face. She lifted her hand and carefully smoothed his brow, her finger trailing slowly down his cheek before it fell away. Her touch was a path of fire.

"Oh," she said.

She shimmied out from between his body and the counter behind her. She pulled her blouse up around her shoulders, gripping the edges in front of her breasts. He had to bite his lip to keep from begging her not to hide herself from him. He watched her carefully, lust surging through him in waves. But with Phoebe, it wasn't merely lust. He loved her, had loved her for years, and he'd forced himself to ignore it, to keep her firmly in the category of friend. The list of reasons—she'd been too young at first, then she wasn't a shifter and all of his baggage about that—felt inconsequential now. The only thing that mattered was the humming pulse of electricity arcing between them.

Her eyes held confusion and concern. "Jake, this is…a lot. You're one of my best friends, and you've said for years that you'd never be with a woman who wasn't a shifter. I'm not a shifter. I can't risk our friendship over a night when you're tired and not thinking straight. Because the thing is, if we go further, I don't know if we can go back."

He closed his eyes and took a deep breath, reining his body in. He didn't want to stop, but he knew she had a point. He was beyond tired and felt rattled inside from recent events. He opened his eyes and met hers. He took another step, pausing in front of her again. He brushed a loose curl out of her eyes, tucking it behind her ear.

"Okay. We'll do this your way for tonight. I might be tired, but it doesn't change the fact that I've wanted you for too long."

Phoebe held his gaze, uncertainty flashing in hers. She nodded slowly. "You'll probably come to your senses after you get some sleep," she said wryly.

Jake traced her lips with his finger, savoring the hitch in her breath. "I finally came to my senses now. Take my word for it. This is only the beginning."

Chapter 2

Phoebe walked to her car, snow crunching under her feet with each step. Snow had fallen again last night. The Maine woods were lovely, almost otherworldly, in the winter. The boughs of balsam and cedar trees were heavy with snow. The bare branches of oaks, elms and other hardwoods stood stark against the sky. A few stubborn leaves clung to the trees, their color faded, though bright against the white backdrop. She paused by her car and looked around. Snow created a soft, muted sense to the forest. A crow called, another answering quickly, their voices clear in the quiet. The sun was cresting in the sky, the snow sparkling where its light touched.

Driving in to work, her mind traveled back to last night with Jake. She'd driven him home, the car charged with electricity arcing between them. She was still stunned at what happened. After years of shoving her feelings for him into a tiny corner of her heart, never to be examined, never to be acted upon, he'd shattered the door to that hidden corner. His kiss, the feel of his hands on her body, and his words had been thrilling and terrifying at once. She couldn't quite believe he'd wanted her for years though he insisted he had. Part of her was frantic to take what he offered. Another part of her was frightened she'd lose one of her best friends if she acted on her desires. Years of hearing Jake's confident proclamations that he couldn't consider being with a woman who wasn't a shifter rang in her mind.

But, oh, how she wanted him. To hear him say he was tired of denying himself was music to her heart. She pulled up at the hospital and hurried inside. She'd overslept after tossing and turning for most of the night. The interlude with Jake had electrified her, her mind and heart spinning in wild circles until she finally fell into an exhausted sleep.

"Hey Rosie," Phoebe called out as she walked past the nursing station and pushed through the swinging door into the break room.

"Hey girl!" Rosie's voice swung behind her into the room.

Phoebe quickly tugged her jacket off and stashed it in her locker. She switched out her winter boots for practical clogs. She was braiding her hair when Rosie entered the room a few minutes later. Rosie walked to the small round table in the center of the room and sat down with a sigh.

"It's not even nine yet, and I'm exhausted. Brought you a coffee," Rosie said.

Phoebe snapped an elastic band around the end of her braid and joined Rosie at the table.

"Ooh, you didn't just get me coffee, you stopped by Roxanne's and got my favorite. Thank you!" Phoebe took a swallow of the rich coffee from Roxanne's, closing her eyes and savoring the flavor. When she opened them, she looked across at Rosie. Rosie was a good friend. They'd met in nursing school. Rosie had grown up in a nearby town and moved to Catamount when she got a job at the local hospital. She was like Phoebe, in that she was distantly related to some shifters, but wasn't one herself. Rosie had short, curly golden hair with bright blue eyes. She looked sweet and innocent, but her mischievous smile gave away her sly sense of humor.

Rosie ran a hand through her curls and eyed Phoebe. "Any word from Shana?"

Phoebe shook her head. Phoebe loved the fact that she got to work with two of her closest friends, Rosie and Shana. But lately, she and Rosie mostly worried about Shana, unsure how to help other than to simply be there however they could. Shana had yet to return to work since her husband, a shifter, died on a highway in Connecticut for reasons that remained mysterious. After staying with Phoebe for a few weeks, Shana had insisted she needed to try to be on her own again and moved into a small guesthouse on her brother's property.

"She's on the schedule for tomorrow," Rosie said. "I'm hoping it'll be good for her to have something to focus on other than Callen's death and everything else that's been going on."

"I think it'll help her. She needs to get out of her head for a bit. I wish this mess would blow over, but it's not looking like it will anytime soon."

Rosie shook her head slowly. "Far as I can tell, the mess has only begun."

"How much worse could it get?"

Rosie threw a hard glance her way. "Um, let's see. Callen died on a highway in mountain lion form. No one knows why the hell he didn't shift back. Then Jake stumbles onto the bombshell that Callen was working with God-only-knows-who to sell the services of Catamount shifters to smuggle drugs. As if that wasn't bad enough, Chloe gets kidnapped by some shifter from out of town and Callen's little brother. Let's not forget that Chloe just happens to be the woman Dane fell head over heels in love with. Dane who's from one of the oldest known shifter families in Catamount and Shana's brother. He's so close to the middle of this, I don't know how he stands the heat. Thank God, Dane and Jake handled Chloe's kidnapping as fast as they did! So, if you're wondering how much worse it could get, I'm thinking we've got a long way to go before this is over."

Phoebe groaned. "I know, I know, I know. I was trying to convince myself it couldn't get any worse. But it's bad. I wish there was something I could do to help."

Rosie sipped her coffee. "Be the good friend you are and just be there. Shana needs you and Jake needs you."

The intercom beeped. "Give me the quick update from rounds this morning," Phoebe said, referring to the early-morning medical rounds that occurred prior to her shift starting.

After a summary of nothing out of the ordinary, Rosie dropped a little bombshell. "Oh, and the new guy here—we think he's a shifter trying to hide it."

Anxiety coiled inside. "What are you talking about?" Phoebe asked in a hiss.

Rosie glanced around quickly. "New patient. He says he's here on vacation and having chest pains. But he feels like a shifter to me. He's in the room at the end of the hall. Check on him and let me know what you think."

Though Phoebe wanted to run down the hall and immediately scope out the man Rosie mentioned, she forced herself to act normal. After doing her usual check-ins with patients from the day before, she made her way down the hall. She found the man in question sitting up in bed watching a cooking show on television. At a glance, she'd have guessed him to be a shifter. Though she wasn't one herself, she'd lived her entire life in Catamount surrounded by them. There were the obvious signs, such as the cat-like eyes and a feline cast to his face. Along with the less obvious signs, such as a distinct feline quality to the way the man lounged in bed and the subtle primal quality to the way he looked at her. In a flash, she recalled Jake's bright blue eyes last night when he'd pulled back from their kiss—dark with passion, a focus so intense it sent shivers up her spine just thinking about it.

"Excuse me?" the man asked.

Phoebe realized she'd zoned out and turned her attention back to the man. He had dark blonde hair and slate gray eyes. She made a point of checking his medical chart by the bed and checked his vitals. The name on the chart was Paul Malone though Phoebe's 'uh-oh' radar was so strong, she doubted that was his actual name. Nonetheless…

"So Paul, how are you feeling today?" Phoebe asked as she entered his blood pressure rating in his chart.

"Okay, I guess. Yesterday was pretty scary."

Phoebe watched him as the man launched into a vague summary of his physical state, increasing her doubt that he had anything wrong with him. But she listened and observed, wondering if Rosie's suspicions were correct, and if so, what would he want by checking himself into the hospital. Phoebe's primary concern was that he was after information on any one of the many shifters who worked in the hospital. Shana was a nurse while her brother Dane was one of the back-up emergency room doctors. They were only two of many shifters who were in and out of the hospital throughout the week.

"So, you said you were visiting Catamount. How

long do you plan to be here?" Phoebe asked after Paul finished talking.

Paul's gray eyes bounced to the window and back to her before he replied. "Not sure. I heard it was a nice place. Thought I'd check it out."

Though Catamount saw its share of visitors in the spring, summer and fall due to its proximity to the Appalachian Trail and its extensive orchards, visitors in winter were much less likely. There was a ski lodge in a nearby town, which tended to draw most of the winter visitors. Phoebe couldn't help herself. "This time of year doesn't bring too many tourists here. Do you have family nearby?"

Paul's eyes tightened, but he kept his expression bland. "I like winter. No reason not to visit just because of that." He turned his focus back to the television, the message loud and clear that Phoebe was dismissed.

Later that afternoon, she walked outside with Rosie after their shift was over. "Well, I'm with you on that guy. I'd bet money he's a shifter. Why is he here and why this hospital? I'm stopping by Jake's office now, and I'll make sure this gets passed on to Hank and Dane."

Rosie climbed into her car with a wave. "Call me if you hear anything. See you tomorrow."

Phoebe headed directly to Jake's office. As soon as she walked in, desire slammed into her body, disorienting her. All of her promises to herself that she'd be able to put their kiss behind her went up in smoke. Jake was looking at his computer screen and ran a hand through his hair. He didn't appear to have heard her come in. For a moment, she allowed herself to enjoy the sight of him. Even hunched over a desk, his body was pure masculinity. He wore a soft t-shirt that stretched across his back, the corded muscles along his spine standing out, his strong shoulders taut under the fabric. She wanted to walk over and drop a kiss on the soft spot where the curve of his neck met the bulk of his shoulder.

He suddenly straightened and swiveled in his chair, his eyes snapping to hers instantly, his intense blue gaze igniting sparks inside of her. Less than five seconds had passed, and her breath was short, molten heat swirled in her center, and she lost focus. It didn't help that Jake's eyes darkened the moment he saw her, desire flashing in them. His primal gaze set butterflies amassing in her belly.

"Hey," he said gruffly.

"Hey." Her one word greeting hung in the air, as she stood frozen inside his office.

All the reasons why she'd kept her feelings for Jake tucked tightly in a corner raced through her thoughts. She forced her eyes away from his, tracking the movement of a cardinal outside flitting in the trees. Its bright red plumage glowed amidst the snowy skeleton of the trees. This is what she'd wanted to avoid—the discomfort, and the worry that he saw the depth of her feelings for him beyond the heat of the moment. Above all, he was one of her best friends. If she lost his friendship, she would be devastated. She was startled out of her train of thought by his voice.

"Phoebe."

The cardinal flew from one branch to another, and she brought her eyes back to Jake. Her belly did a somersault. She couldn't seem to force her body to obey her. Years and years of habit should have kicked in, but the kisses they shared last night had blown her control to bits.

"Whatever you're thinking, stop it," Jake said flatly.

His stark words had the intended effect of knocking her mind off its loop. "How about you stop trying to read my mind?" she countered, irritated at how easily he could read her.

He stood from his chair and moved fluidly around his desk coming to a stop in front of her. He leaned his hips against the desk and reached for her hands, which were cold from the snow-chilled air. The feel of his warm, strong hands around hers caused her breath to draw sharply. Her pulse went wild again, but she couldn't have looked away from his gaze if she wanted.

His hair was rumpled as if he'd run his hands through it repeatedly. His eyes were still tired, though not as weary as they'd been yesterday. Her heart tumbled. The worry she held for him had been constant ever since news had come about Callen's death. None of them could have realized that event was only a harbinger of more to come.

Jake rubbed his thumb across the back of her palm. "I wasn't trying to read your mind. How about we agree not to freak out about last night?"

Relief washed through her. Jake understood. He was trying to get them back on friends-only footing, which was exactly where they needed to be. On the heels of relief came a sharp pain, the pain she'd been trying to avoid for years. A less than five-minute span last night, and the heartbreak she'd tried to avoid for years was in front of her. Because dammit, he'd give her a reason to hope. And no matter how many times she told her heart it wasn't a good idea to hope, her heart ignored her.

Phoebe nodded. "Right. I'm all about not freaking out about last night. It was an aberration. We're friends, we've been friends for years and that won't change."

He shook his head slowly. "That's not what I meant about not freaking out."

Her belly flip-flopped. "What…what did you mean?"

"I meant let's not freak out about what happened because it's absolutely okay. We kissed because we wanted to. I plan to kiss you again…"

Her breath whooshed out of her lungs, and her pulse ricocheted wildly. For a second, her heart flew with joy and longing streaked through her. On the heels of that, she tried to talk her feelings down. She couldn't let herself think this could be real. It hurt enough to pretend her feelings didn't exist, it would be far, far worse to water them with false hopes. "Jake, we can't…"

His thumb stilled its soft strokes. His eyes narrowed, pinned to hers. "Who says we can't?"

When she opened her mouth to reply, Jake released one of her hands and put his finger to her lips. "Tell me you didn't want that kiss," he said, his voice gruff.

Phoebe tried to form the words to tell him she hadn't wanted that kiss, but she couldn't because it was an out and out lie. She closed her eyes and took a deep breath. When she opened them again, Jake's finger traced the contours of her mouth before his hand fell away. Her lips tingled at his soft touch.

"Okay. So now that we got that out of the way, what brings you here?" he asked with a small smile.

She couldn't help the smile that bloomed in her heart, her lips following suit. Just when she thought he was going to push too far, he backed off easily and gave her the emotional space she needed.

"Oh yeah, I came by to tell you we think we have a shifter who checked himself into the hospital."

Jake arched a brow. "And that would be a problem, why? Half the people in town are mountain lion shifters."

"He's from out of town and damn vague. Says he came for a visit and had chest pains yesterday. Rosie saw him first before I got to work and then I checked on him. He's laying low, but I have a bad feeling. I can't think of anything other than bad reasons for him to want to be in the hospital. Shana and Dane both work there, not to mention that plenty of other staff are shifters. We need to talk to Hank and Dane."

Jake swore and dropped her hands. He leaned backwards on his desk and snatched his phone up, making two calls in quick succession. He left messages for Hank and Dane to call right away and set his phone down. He turned back to her.

"Okay, here's the deal, none of you are to be alone with him. We don't know who he's working with, or who he's after. Once I talk to Hank, I'll see if he can set up a security rotation. How long will he be at the hospital?"

"That's the thing, there's no good reason to keep him, but he keeps reporting vague symptoms that we have to run tests on. I think it's better if he's there because we can keep an eye on him."

Jake nodded. "Definitely. Dammit! I was hoping whoever was connected to Seth and Randall would want to stay away after what happened with Chloe. I mean, Seth and Randall are in jail and won't be going anywhere else soon." He pushed away from the desk and began pacing. "You're going to have to keep a close eye on who goes in and out of that room. That might help us sift through who's working with them here in Catamount." He paused and looked at her for a long moment. "Promise me you won't go in his room alone again. For all we know, they're targeting anyone close to those they're after. You're close to Dane, Shana and almost everyone important in the shifter families here. Promise me."

Phoebe nodded. "I promise. Rosie and I already talked about it after I saw him today." Cold fear chased up her spine, and she shivered, hugging her arms around her waist. She caught Jake's eyes. "I wish we knew more."

He stopped pacing in front of her and leaned against

the desk, tugging her into him. Before she could think, he'd wrapped her in his strong, sure embrace. The heat of his body seeped into hers. She leaned her forehead against his shoulder with a sigh. Between the ever-present state of vigilance she'd been in ever since Chloe had been kidnapped and weeks of worry about everything, she was relieved to soak in his reassuring warmth and comfort.

Chapter 3

Jake studied the grain of wood in the floor inside the police station. The building was centuries old and retained the original hardwood oak flooring, worn from years of feet traveling across it, yet still rich in color. Dane was on the phone with Chloe while they waited for Hank. Dane finished his call and slipped his phone in his pocket. He glanced to Jake.

"Every time I think about the mess Callen created, I wish he was still alive so I could make him pay," Dane said, shaking his head, his eyes weary and angry at once.

Jake leaned his head against the wall behind his chair and sighed. "You and me both. How's Chloe?"

"She's good. She's getting annoyed with me checking in all the time, but she's putting up with it so far." Dane paused, his eyes darkening. "I'm relieved she's okay, but I'm not going to breathe easy until we get to the bottom of this."

The door to Hank's office opened and he waved them inside. "Come on in, guys."

Jake and Dane sat in two chairs across from Hank's

desk. Hank took a swig of coffee and turned his gaze to Jake. "So what's up at the hospital?"

Jake quickly filled them in, along with the latest update from his online forays. "I'm thinking one of us needs to head to Montana. As it stands, we're on the defensive on this side while they keep showing up here. Let's get out in front. I've found enough clues online to point us to the right locations. Hell, I can pinpoint the locations of every ISP address linked to the accounts Callen was emailing. Maybe they're fronts, but everything leads somewhere."

Hank glanced between Jake and Dane and shrugged. "I'm with you there, but I can't go. It's gonna have to be someone else. Hate to say it, but we can't send either one of you. You're too prominent. Plus, if they didn't know your faces before, they do now. Both of you were all over the news after Chloe's kidnapping."

Dane swore and looked to Jake. "Any ideas?"

Jake shook his head. "Not yet. Let me think on it."

They moved on to developing a plan for surveillance at the hospital. It twisted Jake's gut that every time they considered the threats shifters were facing, they came face to face with the reality that Callen had recruited within the Catamount Clan. His youngest brother, Randall who'd always been eager to impress Callen, was an easy mark, but they couldn't assume others weren't involved. Sussing out whom they could trust was a complicated task.

Jake walked outside later to find snow drifting down. The police station was in the center of town on one of the streets adjacent to the town green. He crossed the street and walked onto the path that led to the center of the green, leaving footsteps in the fresh layer of snow. It was late afternoon with the sun low in the sky. The bare tree branches cast a network of shadows on the snow. The plump snowflakes glittered as they drifted through the lingering rays of sun angling across the green. He thought of Phoebe, his heart feeling a primal tug. He turned on his heel and walked quickly back to his truck. He needed to see her. *Now.*

As he drove toward her house, a corner of his mind tried to remind him why he'd told himself he'd only be with a shifter. His college girlfriend, Naomi, had been the one and only woman he'd been involved with who wasn't a shifter. He'd fallen so hard and fast for her, he'd ignored the warning signs. She'd been overly dramatic and often portrayed herself as a victim of any number of circumstances. Jake's hormones found her so phenomenal, he'd charged ahead, thinking she needed someone like him and enjoying the superficial pleasure derived from feeling like her hero. In a haze of hormonal overdrive, convinced they were meant to be together, he'd told her who and what he was. She'd promptly gone into drama central mode and flipped out. He'd spent months clearing up rumors and feeling like a complete idiot. The saving grace had been she'd transferred to another college in the aftermath. To this day, he didn't know if she'd done so because she was legitimately afraid of him because he was a shifter, or because she hadn't counted on how many friends he and the other shifters had who were willing to close ranks around them.

He'd stayed true to his commitment to only get involved with shifters since then, but he'd yet to find anyone who called to him. Except Phoebe. She'd always had a straight line to his heart. When he was younger and watched her grow into the beautiful woman she'd become, he'd told himself he couldn't take advantage of her. She was four years behind him in school. The yawning gap between their ages then was nothing now with him at thirty-four and Phoebe at thirty. Between the time he tried to keep from fawning all over Phoebe and his messy brush with Naomi, he never managed to wipe out the shimmering electric connection that hummed to life every time he was near Phoebe.

He might not be thinking too clearly right now, but he was damn tired of denying himself what he wanted. Especially when, in the midst of the suspicions running high in Catamount, Phoebe was one of the few who held his absolute faith. He turned into the driveway to her house in the wispy light of dusk. Her house was a cape style home, painted a soft cream with the whimsical touch of purple trim and a matching purple steel roof. Snow was falling more heavily now, coating the landscape. Phoebe's car wasn't in the drive yet, so Jake texted her quickly asking when she'd be home. Moments later, she replied to report she was on her way. He leaned his head back and watched the snow float down over the field beside her house. A small creek meandered through the field, the dark ribbon of it glimmering under the last rays of sun.

Phoebe's holiday lights came on. Jake chuckled to himself, realizing she must have them set on a timer. Her home was laced with holiday lights along the roof with two bare trees flanking her front walk decorated as well. Phoebe pulled up and waved at him from her car. He climbed out and followed her down the snow-covered slate path to her front entrance. When she reached the door, she turned to him. Her dark hair was flecked with snowflakes. One caught on her lashes, glittering bright under the lights by the door.

"I didn't know you were stopping by," she said, a question in her eyes.

She blinked and the snowflake on her lashes disappeared. Her dark eyes met his, and his breath hitched.

"I hope you're not planning to ask me to leave."

She shook her head and tugged her keys out of her purse. "Of course not. Come on in."

She nudged the door with her shoulder once she unlocked it. Jake's eyes fell to the flimsy lock on her door. He needed to beef up the locks on her house. In Catamount, it had never crossed his mind to worry about the state of anyone's locks. He hated that he had to think this way, but right now all he wanted was to make sure those close to him were safe. They'd gotten lucky with how quickly they'd been able to handle Chloe's kidnapping. He didn't want to be caught blindsided again.

He shut the door behind him and locked it. Phoebe dropped her purse and bag on the couch as she walked into the kitchen, flicking on lamps along the way. The air was cool. He glanced at the woodstove in the corner of her living room.

"I'm going to start a fire, okay?" he called out.

She leaned her head around the archway leading into the kitchen. "Please do," she said with a grin.

Jake eyed the small wood rack nearby and turned to head outside. In the snowy almost-dark, he headed for the woodshed on the side of her yard. Walking through the light cast from her festive holiday lights, he methodically stacked wood on the holder outside her front door, filling it to capacity before bringing an armful inside. Once he had the fire started in the woodstove, Phoebe called to him from the kitchen. He walked in to find her ladling stew into bowls, instantly handing him one when he stepped to her side.

"I made it in the slow-cooker this morning. I didn't know the weather would be ideal for beef stew," she said.

She nudged him to the table and followed him over with a bowl. Jake uncorked the bottle of red wine on the table and filled the wineglasses she'd set out.

"This is amazing," he said a few minutes later between bites of the rich, savory stew.

Phoebe grinned. "I didn't know you'd be enjoying it with me, so I'm glad you like it."

"Not that there'd be any doubt. You're a damn good cook," he replied. He'd shared many meals with Phoebe and knew her to be ridiculously good at cooking and baking. She didn't go for fancy, but could make the simplest meals amazing. He finished his bowl and pushed it away. Leaning back in his chair, he looked over at her. Her dark curls were damp from the snow, her cheeks flushed. Her dark eyes drew him into their depths. All the years he'd known her, he'd vigilantly shut his brain off when it came to thinking about what it would feel like to experience the passion she exuded. She approached most everything with zeal—cooking, hiking, sewing, nursing, and more. With her dark hair and eyes, curvy figure and warm smile, he'd spent years longing to know her beyond the friendship they shared.

Watching her now, he let go of the tight control he'd kept on his feelings for her. He simply didn't care to hide them anymore. He sensed she didn't quite believe him, but he didn't know what to do about that other than show her. When she stood to carry dishes to the sink, he followed her with the empty wineglasses. The clink of dishes and silverware placed in the sink echoed in the quiet room.

Jake's body was humming. After so many years of tamping down the ever-present arc of desire for Phoebe, to allow it to exist freely set him afire. After handing her the wineglasses and feeling the brush of her fingers against the back of his palm in the tiny exchange, he had to close his eyes to keep from yanking her against him. When she finally turned to him, he reached for her hands. Her dark eyes widened, but she didn't say anything. He began walking backwards, drawing her with him into the living room. The light from the fire in the woodstove flickered through the glass door. Snow was still falling outside, the white flakes shining brightly in the glow from the holiday lights encircling the house.

He backed up until his legs bumped the back of the couch. Resting his hips on the edge, he tugged her close, barely able to keep himself under control. The act of letting go of his iron control on his feelings for her was unnerving. The cat in him purred and growled softly, desperate to unleash the lust surging through him. He lifted a hand and trailed the back of it down her cheek, into the soft dip of her neck, across her collarbone and over the lush curve of her breast. Her breath hitched. He flicked his eyes to her face to see her tongue dart out to moisten her lips. The thin thread of control loosened further.

***

Phoebe's body was on fire, molten heat building in her center, slick moisture between her thighs, and a longing for Jake that ran so deep it shook her to her core. When he'd texted her tonight and said he was waiting for her to get home, she'd decided she wouldn't try to turn him away. Desperate as she was to keep her heart safe, she was more desperate to give free rein to her feelings for him. Her body had been simmering ever since he'd kissed her, desire thrumming and pulsing with every breath. Though she seriously wondered if her heart could handle it if she gave in to what she'd wanted for so long and it was torn away from her later. Jake slid his hand around her waist and drew her to him, bringing his lips to hers swiftly. As with the kiss the other night, the feel of his mouth against hers was sheer heaven. Her mouth opened to his and he delved in, seeking, stroking, and tangling.

Her pulse leapt, the desire that had been buzzing in her veins for days blew into a flash-fire through her body. Inside, she was hot, needy, and achy for more. She pressed against him, running her hands up over his shoulders and down the muscled length of his back. He tore his lips from hers, nipping her earlobe, tracing a burning path of kisses down her neck into the dip of her blouse. Shivers raced through her body. He tore at her shirt, a button flying loose and pinging on the floor. She ran her hands under the edge of his cotton shirt. His lips never breaking contact from her skin, he reached a hand behind his head and tugged his shirt up and over in one swift move.

She groaned at the feel of his warm skin under her hands. She'd seen him shirtless countless times over the years—watching him run track in college, swimming in Catamount Lake—and always wondered how good it would feel to touch him. He was all lean muscle and pure strength. His muscles shifted and flexed under her hands. She groaned at how good it felt to touch him. His skin was burnished gold in the flickering light from the fire.

Jake's hands were warm, strong and sure, coasting over her skin in soft touches. He pulled back, his hands on the curve of her hips, his blue eyes dark as he looked at her. He held her eyes as he reached around, and with a flick of his finger, unhooked her bra. The straps slid down her shoulders, her breasts fell loose, heavy and aching for his touch. The air around them was hot and electric, vibrating with the intensity of want and desperate need.

"Phoebe…" he whispered, a hint of reverence in his voice.

She closed her eyes, the moment, the sound of his voice something she'd wanted for so long and beyond what she could have imagined. When he whispered her name again, she opened her eyes and met his, startled at the bare desire reflected in them. She opened her mouth to speak, but groaned when he leaned forward and closed his mouth over her nipples. His tongue swirled, his teeth nipped, and pleasure streaked through her as she arched back with a soft cry. After he gave the same attention to her other breast, she was frantic. She pushed against him, relishing the feel of his hard chest against her soft curves.

The rest of their clothes were torn off in a rush. Time was suspended. Somehow, she found herself pressed against the couch, Jake's hand holding her wrists in his grasp. She was stretched beneath him, her hips rolling against him, blind with need. She struggled to get closer, gasping as the hard planes of his chest caressed her breasts. His free hand coasted over the curve of her belly, sifted through her dark curls and into the drenching moisture of her folds. His lips pulled away from hers slowly, his eyes landing on hers in the shadowy room.

"You feel so good…" His voice was ragged, slurred.

"Jake…please…" Her hips communicated what her voice couldn't when she shifted against his hand.

He slid a finger into her channel. She was so close to the edge, pressure gathered inside. Another finger joined the first, stretching her. Sensation rolled through her in waves, centering on the feel of his fingers in her slick core. She tumbled into the blur of his blue gaze, unable to look away until his lips fell to hers in a searing kiss. He ravaged her mouth, his lips tearing away as he licked his way down her neck. He caught her earlobe in his teeth, the sharp bite sending shivers wracking through her. His fingers pumped in and out of her, driving her to a point of desperation. She distantly heard her voice gasping his name, pleading. His hard, muscled body was fluid under her hands. Rolling her hips against him, sharp pleasure spiked through her as her climax crested, so intense, it tore through her with wave upon wave. She felt his fingers go still inside of her, her channel throbbing around him.

Opening her eyes, she found his on hers—dark and intent. For a flash, she felt self-conscious at her complete abandon in his arms. She shoved the feeling away. Now that they'd broken through this barrier, she would take all she could get. She wanted more. She reached between them, curling her hand around the heated, hard length of his shaft. His forehead fell to hers. She held him in her grip, stroking up and down. His breath hissed when she arched up and left a trail of wet kisses on his neck, nipping at the curve. In a swift move, he reached for his jeans, which had fallen to the floor. Within seconds, he rolled a condom on and brought his eyes back to hers.

Settling his hips against hers, he arched into her, sliding his hot length against her. Just when she thought she'd regained a fraction of control, he drove her beyond wild again, teasing her as he dragged his cock back and forth through her wet folds without giving her what she wanted. He nudged her closer and closer to the edge. Just when she thought she could take no more, he finally surged into her slick heat. He filled her completely, stretching her channel. It had been years since she'd had sex, so she gasped at the fullness, teetering on the edge of pain.

Jake held still for a long moment, his eyes locked to hers. He leaned on his elbows and laced his hands in hers and began to move. In slow, tantalizing strokes, he notched her higher and higher into an arc of pleasure. His hot length filled her again and again. She curled her legs around him, pulling him so close against her, they moved as one. His hands pinned hers by her head as he rocked deeper and deeper into her. She felt surrounded by his body, encompassed in dizzying passion and intimacy at once. Shudders began in her center and spiraled outward until she finally tumbled over the edge again, climaxing around him. His back arched as he surged deeply into her one last time. She felt the pulse of him inside her, her channel throbbing with her lingering climax as his brought his body to a tense arch before he collapsed against her with a growl.

They lay still in the quiet, breathing in rhythm. As reality settled into her awareness, Phoebe couldn't believe she was lying here with Jake inside of her, skin to skin. He shifted his weight to the side and leaned on one elbow. She opened her eyes to find his locked on her. He stroked a stray lock of hair away from her forehead. Uncertain what to say, she simply watched him. She wasn't ready for this moment to end, but was afraid if she said anything, it would shatter the bare intimacy between them.

Jake took a deep breath, his mouth curling in a small smile. He leaned forward and brought his lips to hers in a lingering kiss. When he pulled away, he gave her a long look as his palm rested warm on her belly, his thumb idly stroking her. Without a word, he untangled himself from her and lifted her in his arms, striding down the short hallway off the living room into her bedroom.

Moments later, they were cocooned in her down quilt after he'd stepped into the bathroom and disposed of his condom. His warm heat surrounded her. She thought she should say something.

"Jake?"

He was resting against the pillow with her tucked close against his side. He opened his eyes, meeting hers. "We can talk, but only if you promise not to start questioning what just happened."

"But…"

"But what? We already had the discussion. I've

wanted you for years, and I'm tired of denying it. If you're about to tell me what happened isn't what you wanted, I won't believe you," he said flatly.

Phoebe looked at him for a long moment. She couldn't lie to him, but she still couldn't quite wrap her brain around what he was saying. For once in her life, she decided to stay in the moment. In the soft quiet, she nodded slowly and rested her head on his shoulder. They fell asleep like that—her legs tangled in his, his palm stroking up and down her back slowly until it stilled when he fell asleep.

Chapter 4

Jake shoved his hands in his pockets and tugged the hood from his jacket over his head. He was walking through the hospital parking lot and the early winter wind whipped across the wide-open lot. He stepped into the rotating entry door, relishing the warmth once he stepped into the hospital. No matter the time of day, the hospital buzzed with activity. It wasn't even eight in the morning and the place was bustling. Jake headed to the elevator to the nurses station on the second floor. Phoebe and Shana worked in the general area where patients who came in through the emergency room needed to stay longer, but didn't meet the criteria for the specialized units.

He intended to pose as a repairman and would pretend to do some basic repairs on the windows in the room for the man Phoebe and Rosie thought was a shifter and at the hospital on false pretenses. Rosie met him when he stepped off the elevator. She smiled brightly, her blonde curls and warm blue eyes instantly eliciting a smile in return.

"Hey Rosie."

"Perfect timing," she said, quickly escorting him to the break room where Phoebe had stored a toolbox for him. He'd gone over this plan yesterday with Dane and Hank and reviewed it with Phoebe. They'd collectively agreed it was best if Phoebe wasn't anywhere near him when he came to the hospital. Jake didn't know if he could hide the effect she had on him, particularly if the man was a shifter. Mountain lions were territorial when it came to mates. Jake's feelings for Phoebe would be apparent without a word being spoken. That ran the risk of the man immediately sensing Jake was a shifter and how important Phoebe was to him. If the man didn't already know Jake was a shifter, there was no sense in making it easy for him to find out. The plan was for Rosie to escort him around. They were holding firm to the agreement that whoever this man was, no one would be alone with him.

After Jake tucked his jacket into a locker, he was ready to go. Phoebe had already procured one of the uniforms the hospital maintenance staff wore for him, so he was set. Rosie gestured for him to follow her. They proceeded to move through the rooms, him checking the windows in every room and adding insulation tape anywhere needed. Maine winters were long and cold, so this was a routine repair that no one would question. When they finally entered the room of Paul Malone, Jake moved to the window first, nodding quickly at Paul while Rosie went through the motions of checking his vitals.

Rosie had taken the liberty of tearing off the leftover insulation tape from last winter while Paul had showered yesterday. This gave Jake plenty to do. As Rosie chatted with Paul, Jake casually joined their conversation. Jake knew instantly Paul was a shifter. On the surface, not much gave it away, but the lion in him knew the lion in Paul. And Jake didn't like what he felt. Paul's energy was tight with a tinge of malevolence. Jake didn't know precisely what Paul was after, but he didn't trust his presence in Catamount, and more specifically, in the hospital.

His gut coiled tight with worry for Phoebe. Paul didn't give much away without ever seeming to hide anything either. He casually reported he was from "nowhere and anywhere," claiming he'd been a military brat and never settled anywhere. After Jake maxed his time in the room and it was more than clear they'd get next to nothing out of Paul, he and Rosie headed onto the next few rooms before he returned the toolbox to the break room and made his way out of the hospital.

He'd gotten one glimpse of Phoebe on his way out, which emphatically reinforced why she couldn't have been in the room with him around Paul. The sight of her dark curls, pulled up in a ponytail on top of her head, swinging as she walked around a corner in the hall ahead of him made his heart clench. The sway of her lush hips brought a surge of lust. Years and years of bottled up desire ran wild inside of him. He generally considered himself to be in control when it came to women. With Phoebe, holy hell, he'd lost all control. It had taken *all* of his willpower not to chase her down the hall and pin her against the wall for a kiss.

***

Phoebe pushed through the door into Roxanne's Country Store, cold air swirling around her in a rush as she quickly closed it. She headed straight for the deli in the back. The scent of fresh baked bread wafted in the air. Roxanne stood behind the counter, pouring a cup of coffee with one hand and taking an order with the other. Roxanne's was a fixture in Catamount. Roxanne's grandfather founded the store and named it in honor of Roxanne shortly after she was born. Roxanne had gone on to inherit it after her parents passed away. Being run by one of the founding shifter families in Catamount had likely helped the store get up and running though its popularity stayed strong as the town grew and included many more residents who not only weren't shifters, but hadn't a clue that shifters existed. Roxanne's ran a thriving business due to good food, good atmosphere and occupying the unique slot of a store that served multiple purposes—grocery store, odds and ends, gas station, and a thriving deli and coffee shop that transformed to a friendly neighborhood bar once the sun went down.

Phoebe was meeting Shana here for a late afternoon coffee break. She leaned against the counter, perusing the specials list on the chalkboard. Roxanne turned to her after she rang up someone else.

"Hey girl, how's it going?" Roxanne asked with a smile. She adjusted the pen tucked into the loose knot of her blonde hair. Roxanne had a sturdy build and exuded common sense. She had a small circle of close friends, of which Phoebe felt blessed to be a part. By virtue of her work and personality, Roxanne also knew more gossip than anyone in town. Her wide smile and warm manner had the side effect of dropping people's guard.

"All in all, pretty good, though the bar is low for good these days," Phoebe replied, her comment a reference to the turmoil in Catamount. Roxanne was on the short list of people Phoebe trusted right now. She was a shifter and intensely loyal.

Roxanne's eyes grew serious. "I'll say. Any news on our friend at the hospital?"

Phoebe shook her head, recalling Jake's 'repair' visit yesterday, which had yielded little information beyond that he shared her opinion the man was a shifter.

Roxanne nodded. "So, what'll it be for you this afternoon?"

"Straight coffee for me."

Roxanne nodded and quickly poured her a cup. After paying, Phoebe sat at a table in the corner. Shana arrived minutes later and joined her. Shana's tawny golden hair hung in a silky fall down her back. Her soft gray eyes held a sadness that had been constant since Callen had died. The news of Callen's betrayal of Catamount shifters had devastated Shana. Shana had been one of Phoebe's closest friends since elementary school. Phoebe wanted to wipe away Shana's pain, but she knew it wasn't possible, so all she could do was try to be there for her.

"So today was crazy at work," Shana said by way of greeting.

Phoebe nodded. "I know. It seems like things have been relentless at work the last few weeks."

Shana nodded and turned to Roxanne who'd approached the table with a cup of coffee.

"I figured I'd just not bother with your order and bring your coffee. You always get the same thing," Roxanne said with a warm grin.

Shana's return smile was small, but genuine. "Thank you."

Roxanne set Shana's coffee down and was off to the next customer when her name was called from the deli counter.

Shana took a sip of coffee and looked over at

Phoebe. "Okay, spill it."

"Spill what?"

"Who's staying in the room at the end of the left wing? You and Rosie practically tripped over yourself making sure I didn't get assigned to rounds for that wing. It's high time everyone stopped tiptoeing around me."

Phoebe eyed Shana, whose expression held a touch of defiance. Everyone close to Shana had been doing all they could to shield her from the constant murmurs about Callen. Phoebe knew it had to stop at some point, but she didn't want to see Shana hurt anymore than she already was. "Shana, no one wants to make this any worse than it has to be. Especially after what you've been through the last few weeks."

Shana straightened in her seat and held Phoebe's gaze, her eyes clear though weary. "It's been hell, but maybe I can help. I had no idea what Callen was up to behind my back, but he was my husband. Maybe I can help figure some of this out."

"Are you sure about that?" Phoebe asked, skeptical it could help her friend to delve into the level of betrayal her late husband had been responsible for before his death.

Shana nodded firmly. "Yes. I'm sickened with what we've learned since Callen died. It doesn't change the fact that I loved him, but I didn't love the man who did what he did. So in a weird way, it's almost easier to accept that he's gone when I realize the man I loved was a façade. What's driving me crazy now is facing what he did and the fact that I was too oblivious to see it. I'd like to help for more reasons than one. I want to make sure Catamount shifters are safe, and I think it will help me get over this if I can be a part of finding the truth."

Phoebe nodded slowly. "Okay, I can see your point. Maybe you should talk to Dane about it if you want to help."

Shana rolled her eyes. "My big brother isn't about to agree to let me be involved. He's in overprotective mode after what happened to Chloe. I have to start somewhere else and then he'll have no choice but to deal with my involvement."

"I'm not sure how you're going to have anything to do with the investigation without Dane knowing about it."

"If you let me help, I will."

Phoebe stared at her incredulously. "And how am I supposed to let you help?"

"For starters, maybe you and Rosie could clue me in on who's hiding out on the left wing, and why Jake was in the hospital yesterday pretending to be a repair guy."

Phoebe sighed and shook her head. She couldn't help the small smile that followed. Though she had her doubts, she didn't doubt Shana would do whatever she could to help. Not to mention that hiding things from Shana, one of her closest friends for years, was next to impossible.

Within the half hour, she'd filled Shana in on her and Rosie's suspicions about Paul, and Jake's repairman gambit to assess the situation himself. Though Shana argued to be allowed to check Paul out herself, Phoebe was against it. She had her own worries about Shana, but she also knew Dane, and by extension Jake, would have a thing or two to say about it. In the back of her mind though, she knew Shana had a right to speak for herself and not be subject to the shield her overprotective brother and others wanted to keep around her.

"No way," Phoebe said, shaking her head firmly. "We have no idea what his plan is, but if you're a part of it, we can't have you risking it."

Shana threw her hands up. "Look, if he knows who

I am, he already knows what I look like. I'm sure he knows I work in the hospital. I say we live by the rule of keeping your friends close and your enemies closer."

Phoebe eyed her, twirling a curl around her finger. "Okay, you have a point. But what's the idea? We're already doing the usual rounds to his room. He somehow manages to keep coming up with vague symptoms that prevent him from being discharged. How will it be different to add you to the cycle?"

Shana shrugged. "No idea, but the more of us he encounters, the more chances we have for him to eventually slip up."

Phoebe nodded. "Fair enough. But you have to stick to the same rules the rest of us have: no going in there alone."

Shana nodded vigorously. "Promise. Okay, that's enough for now. After I see him, I'll tell Dane. He'll freak out, but then he'll back off." She sighed. "I know why he's worried, but I can't just sit at home and wait this out."

"I know. How about you stop by for dinner tonight?"

Shana quickly agreed. They returned their empty coffee cups to the counter and headed outside. Phoebe was walking to her car on the far side of the green when she heard her name. She looked up to see Jake leaning against his truck, which was parked in front of her car on the street. Her heart flew inside, wild with joy no matter how hard she tried to keep herself from hoping. Longing for Jake, loving him for years, and keeping her feelings so tightly under wraps made it decidedly difficult to loosen the hold she had on her hopes and dreams about him.

Jake's tawny hair glinted under the holiday lights circling the green. It had been late afternoon when she'd walked into Roxanne's. In the short time she'd been inside, the sun had slipped further down the sky. The town lights flickered on while a half-moon rose above the trees. The sharp scent of balsam cut through the cold air. Phoebe walked across the green, the snow muffling her footsteps.

Jake's eyes held hers every step of the way, his blue gaze bright in the fading light. Her heart drummed against her ribs, butterflies thronged in her belly, and she kept walking to Jake. She came to a stop a few feet away from him. His eyes crinkled at the corners when he reached out and hooked a finger over her belt. She hadn't bothered to zip up her jacket. He pulled her forward in slow motion, tugging her right into his arms.

She didn't know how to deal with this sudden shift in him—not treating her as his platonic friend, but as a woman who was much more than that to him. Her brain couldn't compute it. But she couldn't have pulled back if her life depended on it. To be wrapped in his warm, strong embrace at the end of a long day at work and under the constant strain of worry was pure heaven.

"Hi," she said, her voice muffled against his fleece jacket.

His chest rumbled with a laugh. "Hi yourself." He leaned back against the truck. She lifted her head and looked up at him.

"How was your day?" she asked.

His eyes sobered. "Busy. No new leads. Just dredging through what we have. How was your day?"

Phoebe shrugged. "It's been busier than usual at the hospital, but nothing new. What are you doing here?"

His eyes crinkled at the corners with his smile. "I saw your car and decided to wait for you. I was hoping I could persuade you to have dinner with me."

Phoebe thought she might melt on the spot, but she had to shake her head. "I invited Shana over for dinner tonight. You're welcome to join us though."

As soon as she spoke, she felt self-conscious. She couldn't even adjust to what Jake insisted—that he'd wanted her for years and what was happening between them was only the beginning—but she certainly didn't know if he wanted anyone to know about them. Nor did she know the parameters of what there was to know. Were they having a fling? Was it something more, much more? She didn't know and knew it wasn't healthy for her to keep moving into this without clarifying these issues with Jake. But she couldn't quite do that now in the middle of Catamount.

Before she could take back her invitation, Jake was nodding. "I'd love to. I haven't seen Shana for more than a few minutes at a time the last few weeks. Should I bring anything?"

"Wine, if you want. I don't know what I'm cooking yet, so I hope you don't mind a surprise there."

Jake grinned. "You're one of the best cooks I know. Anything you make is guaranteed to be good."

He leaned forward and took her lips in a swift and fierce kiss. In less than three seconds, Phoebe thought she might go up in flames. He pulled away, softly nipping her bottom lip as he did. "So, should I come by in about an hour?"

She nodded. Dazed, she climbed into her car and let it warm up for a few minutes after she started it. Her whole body tingled. She touched her fingers to her lips, as if she could hold onto the sensation Jake left behind.

Chapter 5

Jake walked into Phoebe's house and smiled. She'd put up a small Christmas tree in the corner of her living room, a young balsam fir that she'd plant come spring. Insisting on a live Christmas tree was classic Phoebe. She hated the idea of cutting trees down solely for the sake of decorating them and then watching them wither and die. For as long as he could recall, her Christmas trees were live, their root balls soaking in a stainless steel tub camouflaged with red felt. Every spring, she'd find the perfect spot and plant the tree. Her decorations were simple with holiday lights draped around the tree and nothing more. A fire flickered in the woodstove. He followed the sound of Phoebe's voice into the kitchen.

While he'd been driving over, he considered that he and Phoebe hadn't discussed how to talk about their relationship with their many mutual friends. He hadn't considered hiding it, but he figured it was something they should talk about. If it were any friend other than Shana, he wouldn't hesitate to walk in and kiss Phoebe senseless, like he wanted to do every time he saw her, and leave the explanations for later. But with everything Shana had been through, he wasn't so sure she needed to bear witness to the newly acknowledged feelings between him and Phoebe. He told himself he'd find a way to keep his hands off of Phoebe for the duration of dinner. He hoped he could manage.

Phoebe's back was to him when he walked into the kitchen. She was slicing something on the counter. Her hair was tied in a loose knot that fell haphazardly to the side. She wore a soft cotton shirt of bright red fabric that hugged her curves, accentuating the dip at her waist and flare of her hips. He reined in the urge to walk over and kiss the curve of her neck and cup her luscious bottom in his hands.

"Hey Jake, it's so good to see you," Shana said as she stood up from the table.

Jake strode to her side and tugged her into a quick embrace. "How are you?" he asked, pulling back and looking into her eyes.

Shana smiled softly, her eyes tired, but determined. He sensed that she'd decided she was going to face the mess Callen left behind. She nodded firmly. "I'm getting there. I went back to work today."

He stepped back from her when she moved to sit down. "Glad to hear you made it back to work." He paused, wondering what to talk about with her. There was so much happening that linked to Callen, and yet Shana had been left to face his betrayal on her own.

Shana held his eyes. "Don't be afraid to talk in front of me. I told Phoebe I'm tired of everyone tiptoeing around me. Callen died and it's awful. And now I know he wasn't who I thought he was, which makes it all worse. The town's in an uproar, so don't try to act like nothing's going on. The way I see it, it's better if I hear what's happening. Otherwise, I've got a million places I can go in my head, most of them even worse."

Jake considered Shana's words. Ever since he'd stumbled on Callen's betrayal, he'd wondered how Shana was feeling. She was a strong woman, one of the strongest female shifters in the area. He figured Callen's betrayal would sting even more as a result. She'd been a leader in Catamount, alongside Callen. Though she'd been cleared of any involvement in Callen's dealings, there were whispers. Jake knew they stung. It didn't surprise him she'd want to face this head on, that was her personality. He met her eyes and nodded firmly.

Phoebe turned to them, setting the chopping knife on the counter and wiping her hands on a towel. She caught his eyes. A current of electricity pulled taut between them. Jake forced himself to remain where he stood and attempted to smile casually at her.

"Shana wants to help with the investigation," Phoebe said, her eyes holding his. "I think you should let her. She might be able to point us in the right direction. She didn't know Callen was doing what he did, but she might be able to figure out things like what his aliases meant. What do you think?"

Jake forced his eyes away from Phoebe and looked to Shana. "Shana, I don't know if that's such a good idea."

Shana cut him off, her eyes resolute. "Jake, I'm sick to learn about what Callen was doing. Please let me try to help. If you don't trust me, you can watch over my shoulder every step of the way."

Jake shook his head. "Of course I trust you! We all trust you. If you're wondering…"

Shana interjected again. "Since you won't say it, I will. If I were you, I'd be worried about me. Callen was my husband. I loved him, or at least I loved the man I believed him to be. How he hid what he was doing so completely is beyond me. All I knew was he was on his quest to connect with shifters out West. I'm wondering how I could have been so blind. I don't blame you and everyone else for being suspicious." Shana's eyes were bright with tears as she looked between him and Phoebe.

Phoebe moved toward her, and Shana waved her away. She wiped at her tears and took a shuddering breath. Phoebe's eyes caught his, and it was all he could do not to step to her side and pull her in his arms. He knew it pained her deeply to see her friend go through this. He thought it was best to be direct with Shana.

He met Shana's eyes. "I trust you because I've known you forever, and there's no doubt in my mind you had nothing to do with what Callen was doing. But I also made sure to back up my trust with facts. When I stumbled onto Callen's email aliases, I crosschecked every single email he sent with your schedule at the hospital. You were never home when those emails were sent." He glanced at Phoebe, relieved she already knew he'd done this. He had to, not because he didn't trust Shana, but because of the very reason Shana thought people might doubt her. "In case you're thinking I did that because I didn't trust you, think again. I did it because I wanted to make sure no one had reason to doubt you."

Shana held his gaze steadily. "I'm so relieved you did that. I'd rather you did than didn't. I just…" She paused, her breath hitching. "…don't know how I could have fallen for Callen's lies. I'm so angry with him, and he's gone, so I can't do anything about it. I want to go talk to his family, but I don't dare. I'm afraid of what I might say and what they might know. Have you looked into anyone else other than Randall?"

Jake nodded. "We're investigating anyone connected to Callen. I promise you, we'll get to the bottom of this. If you want to help, let's talk to Dane first."

Shana rolled her eyes. "That's what Phoebe said. You know he won't let me anywhere near any of this. He's so freaked out about Chloe getting kidnapped, he's got me giving him my schedule every day."

Jake shrugged. "Far as I'm concerned, that makes sense." If Jake had his way, every woman who mattered to him, family and friends, would stay far away from the mess Callen had left behind. Anger sparked under his skin at the reminder of Chloe's kidnapping.

It was Phoebe's turn to interject. "Are you serious? Jake, Shana can't be expected to report in to Dane every day!"

Jake met Phoebe's eyes, which were flashing with irritation. After Chloe's kidnapping by Callen's younger brother, Randall, and one of Callen's contacts from Montana, Jake had been worried for anyone and everyone connected to shifters in Catamount. His closest friend Dane, of course, was hyper-aware after Chloe was kidnapped. Dane's family was swirling in the center of the storm with Shana his sister and Chloe his fiancée. For Jake, even the passing thought that something could happen to Phoebe knotted fear around his heart. He looked between Phoebe and Shana. He reined in his desire to command them to stay out of this. He knew them both well enough to know that would result in the opposite. It took a massive effort with his protective instincts in high gear, but he bit back his words and forced himself to speak slowly.

"Look, we're worried about everyone. After what happened to Chloe, the last thing anyone wants is for someone else to get kidnapped. We already know about the guy at the hospital." His words stopped when he realized Shana might not know about that. When he looked to Phoebe, she nodded in Shana's direction.

"She knows. We didn't say anything, but she figured it out," Phoebe commented.

Shana rolled her eyes. "As if I wouldn't notice that you all were trying to keep me out of an entire wing on our floor." Looking back at Jake, she continued. "That's my point. Tiptoeing around me isn't helping. It's not like I don't notice. I get why Dane's worried, I do. I just want to try to help if I can."

Jake nodded slowly. "I'll talk to Hank and Dane tomorrow. It's fine with me if you help me sift through the mountain of emails I'm plowing through. You might have some insight into different aliases and maybe Callen dropped some clues about the people he was working with."

Shana nodded quickly. "How about I meet you at your office in the morning?"

"How about we let Dane know first?" he countered. "He'd rather you work with me, if anything."

Shana huffed, but she didn't argue. Conversation moved on. Jake was glad to see Shana, but found dinner highlighted a sad truth. Until he knew Catamount shifters were out of danger, there would be no casual dinners with friends that didn't feel weighted by the threats swirling around. The level of betrayal set in motion by Callen was still on a destructive course. His younger brother waited in jail, holding their secrets close for now. Questions hung everywhere regarding who else might be involved.

If Shana noticed the current buzzing between him and Phoebe, she gave no indication of it. For Jake's part, it was taking all of his discipline to keep his hands off of Phoebe. Over many years of friendship, dinners with Phoebe and any combination of mutual friends had been common. Though he was accustomed to keeping a lid on his feelings, he couldn't have known how difficult it would be once that lid had been blown off.

The mundane activity of helping Phoebe clean up after dinner with Shana present brought his body to the edge of pain. Phoebe's kitchen had never felt so small. The brush of her arm against his, the swing of her hair when it tumbled free, the catch of her breath when he gave in to the urge and swiftly stroked a hand down the curve of her hip when Shana stepped out to go to the bathroom—every tiny moment tightened the coil of desire inside of him.

Phoebe's dark eyes snagged on his as Shana's footsteps approached the kitchen again. He couldn't help himself and closed the space between them, dropping a kiss on the side of her neck.

"Jake, what are you doing?" she whispered fiercely.

He stepped back just as Shana entered the kitchen, savoring the satisfaction that rose in him at the flush staining Phoebe's cheeks.

Shana stepped to the table and picked up her purse, looping it over her shoulder. In moments, she said her goodbyes, assuring Jake she'd be at his office first thing tomorrow. Phoebe followed her to the door. Jake leaned against the wall, watching Phoebe close the door behind Shana. The fire had burned to embers in the woodstove, flickering sparks mingling amidst the soft light cast by the holiday lights on the tree.

Phoebe turned and leaned against the door. Her hair fell in a rumple of dark curls around her shoulders. Her eyes met his, a question held in them. He covered the distance between them in quick strides, answering her unspoken question with a kiss. She gasped when he brought his lips to hers. He'd intended to be gentle, but the second her mouth opened, his kiss turned rough. Touching her set loose the lust that he could barely hold in check anymore. Years of discipline broke down completely. She was the key to his primal desire—calling to both sides of him though his cat simmered under his skin in every moment with her.

He devoured her mouth—deep strokes, soft bites, and unrestrained want galloping through him. His pulse rocketed. He pressed her into the door, imprinting his body against hers, growling softly at the feel of her soft curves against him. He seared a wet path down her neck, coasting his hands up her sides to curl around her breasts, soft and heavy in his hands. He needed to feel her skin, the need so frantic, he tore at her shirt. The next few moments passed in a blur. Clothes were torn off, her soft skin flashed in the dimness, their ragged breathing mingled—until she was bare before him.

She stood leaning against the door, her nipples peaked in the shadowed light, her generous breasts rising and falling with her breath. Her lips were parted, her eyes dark. He stood inches away, his chest bare, his arousal straining against the denim of his jeans. Jake was coming to love the side of Phoebe he saw when she was aroused. Though he'd tamped down many a fantasy of her over the years, his fantasies couldn't have done justice to what she was like. Once the walls of her restraint fell, the passion between them burned so hot and high, he lost himself in it.

She slowly reached forward, hooked a finger in his belt loop and drew him closer. The feel of her hand stroking the length of his arousal through his jeans almost brought him to his knees. Her eyes met his—a hot lick of a look—as she slid his zipper down and pushed him back a step. The warmth of her palm around his cock brought a groan. He tried to say her name, but couldn't. Her breasts swayed as she leaned forward and took him in her mouth. She proceeded to bring him to the edge of a place he'd never been. He was always in control when it came to sex…

always.

But now, with Phoebe's mouth on him, stroking, licking, and sucking, he fell into the hot and electric pulse around them. He looked down to see the arch of her spine as she leaned forward, her skin damp and glistening in the dim light. He slid his hands down her spine, coming to rest at her hips and holding on for dear life as she brought him fully into her mouth again and again. Just when he was on the verge of exploding, she went still and slowly drew away. She stood, eyes pinned to his, desire shimmering in her gaze.

Her skin was dewy with the sheen of desire, her curls a wild rumple around her shoulders. Her pulse was visible in her neck, her breathing ragged. Jake closed the small space between them, lifting her roughly in his arms, turning to the couch and stretching her under him. She gasped as he pressed her back, shifting between her knees and pushing her thighs apart. Lust clawed at him. He ran his palms up her thighs, savoring the give of her skin. He stroked a finger through her wet folds, almost losing it when her hips writhed against his touch. With one hand gripping her hip and holding her still, he brought his mouth to the center of her. He dove into giving her pleasure—deep delves of his fingers into her channel, rough strokes of his tongue as he explored every inch of her. Her cries and gasps fed him, notching the heat inside higher and higher until he was taut with the restraint of holding back. Her body suddenly arched in a shivering stretch as he drew her clit into his mouth, holding suction until she convulsed around his hand. He slowed his movements until her body relaxed, soft shudders reverberating against him.

With a growl, he hooked a hand under her thigh, lifting it swiftly and sliding up into the cradle of her hips as he shoved his jeans down. He fumbled for a condom and rolled it on with his free hand. Her folds were slick against the head of his cock. He grabbed onto a thin thread of control and met her eyes, forcing himself to wait. Her mouth parted, his name falling from her lips in a soft gasp. Only then did he plunge inside of her, growling when he sank to the hilt. The creamy clench of her channel almost pushed him over the edge, but he managed to hold on. Her eyes closed in the fevered passion of the moment.

"Look at me," he commanded softly.

She did, those wild, dark eyes landing on his. Never breaking his gaze, he began to stroke inside her channel. The only thing that kept him from letting go was the promise in her eyes. Only when he felt her begin to throb around him did he let go. She flew apart again, her cries raining down around him as he pounded into her, the unbearable pressure inside of him finally letting loose.

Chapter 6

Phoebe drifted down slowly, the only thing anchoring her the feel of Jake's skin against hers. Pleasure echoed in her body. When she came to full awareness and realized how wanton she'd just been with him, a flush washed through her. She wanted to run and hide, but she couldn't and wouldn't. She opened her eyes to find his blue gaze dark and intent on her.

She took a breath, her breasts pushing against the hard planes of his chest as she did, accentuating the awareness of what his body did to her. Jake held still for a long moment before slowly shifting his hips away and untangling himself from her. Before she could even form a thought, much less move, he'd walked to the bathroom to dispose of his condom and returned to the living room to find her lying exactly where he'd left her.

This…*this*…with Jake was flinging her so far out of her comfort zone she didn't know what to do. Jake tugged his clothes on and picked up her scattered clothing. He sat beside her, his eyes warm and bemused. He ran a hand down her arm. Only then did she realize she was getting cold.

"You're going to freeze," he said, swiftly rubbing both hands up and down her arms, which were pebbled from the chilled air.

She finally broke out of her trance and accepted the clothes he handed to her. Moments later, they were back in the kitchen. She started water for tea, thinking it would give her something to do. Yet waiting for water to boil offered little distraction. Her mind spun over the unraveling of her control. All Jake had to do was look her way and her senses were overcome. She kept telling herself they had to slow down, had to make sure they weren't on the way to blowing up their friendship. Then he touched her, and she went up in smoke. He was seated at the table, his legs stretched out in front of him. She turned to look at him, wondering what to say. Her heart wanted to curl up against him and just *be* with him, while her head wanted to calmly discuss what was happening and what they should do. The confusion between her heart and mind froze her.

He looked up at her. Silence stretched between them. Doubts galloped through her mind. She was so absorbed in worrying about what to say, she jumped when he said her name.

"Huh?"

"Did you hear me the first two times?" he asked.

"Hear what?"

"I've said your name three times now," he said with a soft chuckle.

Jake was far too complacent for her comfort. Though the very thing she'd wanted for so many years was actually happening, she couldn't quite believe it and was terrified if it fell apart, she'd be without one of her best friends.

"How can you be so…so calm?" she asked, pacing

back and forth in her small kitchen.

"Did I miss something? A few minutes ago, you blew my mind again and now you're obviously upset about something. What's going on?"

She threw her hands up, grumbling when the teapot whistled. She quickly turned the burner off and whirled back to face him. "This, this…" She waved her hands around. "…thing with us. We can't just do this. I don't want to mess things up. You're one of my best friends. I don't know where you think things are going. I'm freaking out because I don't get it. Since college, which was over ten years ago now, you've been all about how you'd never be with a woman unless she was a shifter. News flash—I'm not a shifter, never will be a shifter. I'm not going to pretend like what's happening doesn't feel good because I'm not stupid, but I can't take this much longer. We have to talk about what's happening, and we should probably try to slow down."

Jake's eyes widened. "Okay, okay. Let's talk."

Phoebe turned away, blinking back tears. This was too much. She wanted to talk, and she didn't want to talk. Her feelings were riding too close to the surface, too raw and too deep. But she couldn't keep going wild with him. With the invisible barriers fallen between them, even the smallest indication from him and she lost control. She barely recognized herself in the aftermath. But if she insisted they talk, and it led to a stop to this, her worst fears would come true. She couldn't imagine trying to tuck her feelings away for him now, nor could she bear it to let him go with the knowledge that he would eventually find and fall in love with a shifter. Her hand shook as she poured hot water into the two mugs she'd set on the counter. She set the teapot down and breathed in slowly.

Turning around, she carried the steaming mugs to

the kitchen table and sat down across from Jake. She slid his mug across the table and nudged the small container that held a selection of teas in his direction. He was quiet while he snagged a teabag and dunked it in his mug. The warm mug anchored her as she cupped it in her hands. She'd pushed to talk, and now she didn't even know where to start.

Jake's blue eyes met hers, his gaze questioning. When she didn't say anything, he leaned back in his chair, a muscle ticking in his jaw.

"You don't believe what I've already said, do you?"

She took a breath. "You mean the part about how you've wanted me for years?"

He nodded sharply. Anxiety knotted in her chest as she tried to sort through how to explain her worries to him.

"It's not that I don't believe you. I mean…" She paused, a flush racing through her. "…I can tell you want me like that. I just don't know if it's a good idea for us to let this play out. You mean a lot to me. I don't know if I can take it if this is a fun interlude for you, and then we try to go back to being friends. I can't do that. I don't know what to do."

Once she bluntly stated she couldn't do that, she felt simultaneously terrified and relieved. He needed to know she had to put some boundaries around this. But in doing so, she might be putting the brakes on what was happening between them, and she could hardly bear the thought. Her eyes focused on the tiny frog painted on her mug, her vision narrowing until that's all she saw.

"Phoebe," Jake said her name softly.

Her head whipped up, her eyes colliding with his warm blue gaze.

"I think maybe you misunderstood what I meant by wanting you."

"Um, okay. What did you mean by that?" Her heart thudded against her ribcage.

"I meant that I wanted *you*, not just sex. Don't get me wrong, I want you like that too. But more than that, I want us to try to have a chance."

"A chance?" Her heart was about to pound its way out of her chest at this point. Her throat was tight, and she could hardly catch her breath. She felt as if she was leaning forward to fly into something she wanted so badly, she could almost feel it, almost believe it was real. But she couldn't quite see, couldn't quite be certain of what lay ahead.

For the first time, she saw uncertainty in his eyes. He took a breath, his shoulders rising and falling. He rolled his neck side to side and finally brought his eyes to hers again. "A chance at a relationship. I guess I figured that was obvious. You're one of my best friends. I never thought we'd just have sex and that would be it. You're the one woman I've never been able to get out of my mind. I know all the stuff I said about not being with women who weren't shifters. After everything that's happened recently, I've realized it was stupid for me to get hung up on the way things went with Naomi. The last month or so has reminded me that shifters can be just as bad to other shifters as humans can. To make a really long story short, I'm tired of denying how I feel about you. I want you like I've never wanted anyone, but it's about a lot more than sex."

Phoebe could hardly believe what she'd heard. She shook her head, trying to clear the fog in her brain.

Jake reached across the table, hooking his fingers under the edge of her hand and tugging it free from the mug. His big, strong hand curled around hers, his thumb stroking across the back of her palm. "Did you hear me?"

She nodded jerkily. "Uh huh."

"Well?"

"That, um, that helps. I didn't understand you before. I just…" Her words trailed off, her throat tight. A tear tumbled over her lashes, splashing onto her cheek. She swiped at it with her free hand and took a shuddering breath. "This is…a lot. I'm not going to pretend this isn't what I want. It's just a lot to adjust to. I'm worried…"

Jake shook his head sharply. "Don't go there. Don't start this by thinking it won't work. We have something a lot of people never get. You're already one of the best friends I've ever had. I trust you completely. That's where we start. Don't start by thinking it can't work. Please."

Phoebe met his eyes, her heart in her throat. His words were everything she wanted to hear, but she couldn't quite take it in. She needed time to see how it felt. She worried this was all happening because of the crisis simmering and bubbling over around them, and when it all settled down, Jake would remember what he'd wanted to begin with. But she couldn't say no, couldn't conceive of turning away from him. With her heart pounding in her ears, she nodded.

Hours later, she woke during the night. Jake was asleep beside her, their legs tangled together. The wind howled outside. She rolled her head to glance out the window. She'd forgotten to close her curtains before they fell asleep. Snow streaked in the wind, lit up by the lights outside. The winter's first heavy storm swirled around the house. She carefully untangled her legs from his and turned on her side to watch the storm. Jake mumbled and followed her, instantly curling his form around hers—two pieces of a puzzle.

***

"What the hell are you thinking?" Phoebe

demanded.

Shana stood in front of her in the break room at work, her arms crossed, her mouth in a tight line. "That I need to do something! That's what. I just told you what I heard. Hank said he's talked with Dane and Jake about who they can send out to Montana. So, I'm going. No reason not to."

Shana whirled away from Phoebe and quickly stuffed her work clothes inside her locker before yanking her coat and purse out.

Phoebe's mind whirred. She had to stall Shana, but Shana was one of the most stubborn people she knew. Conveniently, Rosie walked into the break room. She quickly glanced between them and stopped at the door, pushing it shut with her hips and leaning on it. She eyed Shana speculatively. "What's up?"

Shana glared at her. "I'm taking a trip."

Rosie slanted her eyes to Phoebe. Phoebe shrugged and shook her head. "Shana thinks she needs to go to Montana to see what she can find out about the shifters out there. It's crazy." Phoebe caught Shana's eyes. "Please listen to me. I'm not saying you can't go. I just think it's better if we actually talk to Hank, Dane and Jake about this. All you did was overhear half of a conversation. Don't do anything rash. That's all I'm asking."

Rosie's eyes widened. "What the hell? Shana, you can't be serious."

Shana's eyes had a wild edge. She glanced between Rosie and Phoebe. "I'm serious, and I refuse to be talked out of it. I can damn well take care of myself and both of you know it."

After several more minutes of futile arguing, Shana shoved past them, pushing the door open and Rosie out of the way. She stalked down the hall. Fear, worry, and anger clashed inside Phoebe. She looked at Rosie. “I can’t let her go alone, but she won’t be stopped.”

Rosie’s eyes mirrored her concern. “I don’t know what to say. I’d offer to chase her down, but she’s more likely to listen to you than anyone else.”

Phoebe grabbed her coat and purse, racing out of the room. She turned to glance over her shoulder before she left. “If I have to, I’m going with her. I’ll try to call Jake, but promise me you’ll call him and Dane.”

At Rosie’s quick nod, Phoebe dashed after Shana.

Chapter 7

Jake kicked his boots against the threshold as he stepped into his office. Over a foot of snow had fallen last night. Catamount was blanketed in fluffy white snow. In Maine, the world barely missed a beat after such a storm. By the time he'd awakened spooned behind Phoebe as the first shafts of sun rose above the trees, the roads had already been plowed. When she'd rolled over in his arms, the flicker of doubt that hung in her gaze reached into his heart. He didn't know how to make her trust how he felt. But he knew her well, and he knew trying to force the issue wouldn't help. She was a person of action. Actions, not words, defined her life. She was the last person to stand up and make proclamations about anything, and yet the first to *do* something to make a difference. She wasn't the friend who would offer platitudes. She was the friend who'd quietly take care of the practical matters for a friend in need, as she'd done for Shana in the early days and weeks after Callen's death.

With that in mind, he decided he'd stop trying to explain her worries away and let his actions show her the truth behind his words. The soft brush of her lips against his sent his pulse rocketing and lust tightening inside. The sound of a snowplow in her driveway interrupted them, and she'd leapt out of bed to race outside and move her car. He'd left her house shortly thereafter, his lust barely in check.

With a sharp shake of his head, he tossed his jacket on the coatrack by the door and immediately sat down at his desk, powering his computer up and diving back into his work. A while later, Dane stepped into his office.

As soon as he met Dane's eyes, his stomach clenched.

"What's that look for?" Jake asked.

Dane's blue-gray eyes were dark, his jaw tight. "Shana just texted me. She and Phoebe are on their way to Montana. That guy Paul at the hospital is gone. He snuck out during the night. Did you fuckin' know this was happening?"

"No! How the hell could you even think I would know about this?" Jake pushed his chair back and stood. He glanced at his desk, trying to find his phone. He spotted it under some loose papers and grabbed it, seeing he'd missed two calls from Phoebe in the last few hours. He'd been so busy with work, he hadn't noticed his phone had been on silent. Fear knotted in his gut, and anger flashed. His cat simmered under his skin. What he wanted was to shift and chase. He fought the urge because he knew he needed to think. "Are you sure? I can't believe Shana and Phoebe would take off like that."

Dane yanked his phone out of his pocket and tossed it to Jake. "Text is right there."

Jake snagged the phone and glanced at the screen. Sure enough, there was a text from Shana. *I'm with Phoebe. We're on our way to Montana. Don't freak out.*

We'll be fine. Visited Hank at the station. He had nothing to do with this. Someone has to check out Montana and it can't be you and Jake, so we're going. Call you when we land.

"What the hell are they thinking?" Jake went to snatch his jacket. "Let's go. We'll follow them."

He quickly listened to the two messages from Phoebe—both explaining that Shana was taking off, and Phoebe thought someone needed to be with her. He swore and threw the phone. It bounced against the wall, and Dane caught it. Jake began pulling his jacket on only to find Dane standing there, arms crossed. "We're talking to Hank first. I already checked their schedule. They won't land for hours yet. Next flight out of Portland to Bozeman isn't until tomorrow. Get on your computer and let's pull up as much data as we can before we sort out who's going after them."

Jake shook his head. "Let's drive to Boston and leave from there. We're not waiting." Fury and fear thrummed through him, fuzzing his thoughts. Thoughts of Phoebe pounded with every beat of his heart. He'd finally let his heart experience what she meant to him, and it ran so deep, he couldn't bear the thought that she might be following Shana into danger. He needed her like the air he breathed.

Dane took a step back and blocked the door. Jake swore savagely and stood toe to toe with Dane, locking eyes with him. He didn't want to shift, didn't want to battle Dane, but he would if he had to.

"What the hell is wrong with you?" Dane asked, placing his palm on Jake's chest and pushing back. "Calm the fuck down. You know we have to think this through. I'm just as worried as you, but…" Dane paused and eyed him carefully. "What is with you?"

Jake forced himself to breathe, reining in the urge to

shift. He could barely contain it, his cat lay so close to the surface. He shook his head sharply. "Nothing's with me. I'm scared for Phoebe and Shana. I'm surprised you're not. These guys always seem to be one step ahead of us. We have no idea who Paul is, or why he was here. After what happened to Chloe, I can't believe you're asking me what's wrong with me."

Dane's eyes sharpened. "Of course I'm worried about Shana and Phoebe! And you of all people should know why I'm saying we should take a little time to think this through before we do anything. That's exactly what you said the day Chloe went missing—that we had to take it one step at a time. That's all I'm saying."

Jake heard Dane's words, but barely. He couldn't shake free the thought that something might happen to Phoebe. He'd finally, finally given in to what his heart and body had wanted for so many years and now he had to face the reality that she could be walking into a trap. When they'd discussed the fact that someone should probably get out to Montana to follow up on the leads they had, he'd never considered it would involve Phoebe. He wanted to talk to her *now*.

Dane cleared his throat.

Jake whipped his head back up to meet Dane's eyes. "What?"

"It's Phoebe. You finally stopped running from how you feel about her."

Jake started to shake his head and then stopped abruptly. Dane was his closest male friend, a brother to him in spirit, as a human and a mountain lion. They'd been together every step of their lives. While they rarely spoke of emotions, he knew Dane felt things deeply. And he knew there was no sense in hiding his feelings from Dane. He took a breath, still wrestling to keep himself from shifting.

The only thing stopping him was Dane's calm presence, and the knowledge that if he tried to battle past Dane when he shifted, it would likely end in a tie.

He looked out the window at the snow coating the ground. The tree outside his office window was glistening with drops of melted snow under the sun. He turned back to Dane and nodded. "You could say that," he said tightly.

Dane nodded firmly. "About damn time. Now it's my turn to keep you sane. You kept me from running off wild after Chloe. You told me not to be stupid, so I'm telling you the same. I've already talked to Hank. We'll go, but first, let's decide where we're starting. Hank's calling in a favor from a friend out there who works for a private security firm. They'll be at the airport when Shana and Phoebe land and won't let them out of their sight. You and I will be right behind them." Dane paused and eyed him. He shook his head with a chuckle. "I wondered when you'd come to your senses. You've loved her for years."

Jake felt as if he'd been punched in the chest, the breath he'd been holding let loose with a groan. "I have. Now I have to make sure she's safe."

Chapter 8

Phoebe threaded through the cluster of people at baggage claim in the airport in Bozeman. Shana had stepped to the other side of the baggage carousel when she saw her bag making its way around. Phoebe quickly snagged her own bag and turned to get out of the way. She met Shana over by a customer service counter.

"Let's rent a car and find our hotel," Phoebe said as soon as she reached Shana's side.

Shana glanced up at her, her blue-gray eyes tired. "Right. I promised Dane I'd call when we landed. Do you mind handling the car rental while I call him?"

Phoebe nodded and glanced around. As soon as she spied the car rental signs, she headed that way, gesturing for Shana to follow her. She fumbled for her phone in her purse and quickly called Jake. Once again, she got his voice mail, so she left another message. She'd tried her damnedest to talk Shana out of leaving for Montana, but after it became abundantly clear Shana was going with or without Phoebe, she reluctantly decided to go with her. She couldn't stand by and watch Shana walk into danger by herself. Phoebe figured the least she could do was try to keep Shana from doing anything too impulsive.

She'd tried to call Jake before they left, but all she'd gotten was his voice mail. She worried he'd misunderstand why she chose to go with Shana. Phoebe shook her thoughts away and strode to the counter. A few minutes later, she tucked the keys to the rental car in her pocket and turned to find Shana leaning against the wall nearby, talking furiously into her phone. When she approached, Shana swore and ended the call.

"Let me guess, Dane's pissed off?"

Shana nodded and began walking. Phoebe followed her, wheeling her suitcase behind her. "So, what did he say?"

"He and Jake are on their way tomorrow," Shana said tightly. "He doesn't get how stupid that is. If the shifters we believe are out here are, in fact, here, there's no way they don't know who Dane and Jake are. Their faces were all over the local news after Chloe's kidnapping. I tried to tell him we'd be careful, but he won't hear it."

They walked the remainder of the way to the rental car in silence. Once Phoebe was driving out of the parking lot, Shana spoke again. "Oh, and Dane said to tell you to call Jake. In fact, he said to tell you he knows what's going on with you two, so you'd better understand why Jake is upset. Mind filling me in on what's going on with Jake?"

Phoebe sighed. She hadn't been trying to hide anything from Shana, but she hadn't had a chance to talk to her either. Every time she thought about it, she hesitated for fear it would hurt Shana because she couldn't imagine Shana watching someone else start a new relationship while sifting through the ashes of her husband's death and the knowledge of his betrayal. The additional complication involved Phoebe's own mixed feelings. She'd loved Jake for years, but she was finding it confusing and confounding to accept the reality that they might have a chance. She couldn't quite trust it.

Phoebe came to a stoplight and glanced at Shana. Shana met her eyes, steady and concerned.

"Jake and I, uh, I guess we're kind of in a relationship," Phoebe blurted out.

Shana's eyes widened slightly and then the corner of her mouth tipped up. "You two have been circling each other for years. How long has this been going on?"

"Not long at all. With everything going on, I guess it just…happened." Phoebe looked away to check on the light. She drove through the intersection, her heart pounding wildly in her chest. Saying aloud what was happening between her and Jake somehow made it feel more real. She took a shaky breath, trying to gather her wits. "I wasn't trying to hide anything from you. So much has been going on…"

Shana interjected. "I'm guessing you've got yourself all worked up about it and didn't know if I could handle hearing two of my best friends finally did something about how they felt. My heart breaks every time I think about Callen dying and the fact that he wasn't who I thought he was. But I would never begrudge you finding your own happiness. You never said a word about it, but it was obvious to me you've loved him for years. What does Jake have to say about all of it?"

Phoebe turned into the parking lot at the hotel once she saw the sign. She waited until she found a parking spot before turning the car off and looking at Shana. "Jake said he's wanted me for years. He said he wants us to have a chance." She paused, her throat tight with tears. She couldn't sort out why, but somehow experiencing intimacy with Jake had twisted her to knots inside. Because if it didn't work out for them, she had no idea how her heart could handle it. "When we're together, it's amazing. You're right that I've loved him for years. But I never talked about it because he swore for years and years that he'd never be with any woman who wasn't a shifter. And now, I'm scared because I don't know if I can take it if things don't work out for us. What if he changes his mind? What if it is best for him to be with a shifter? I don't know what I'll do."

Shana's mouth twisted in a rueful smile. "I may not be the best one to give advice since I hardly trust anyone after what Callen did, but I'll try. The list of people I trust is super short, but you're on it and so is Jake. Jake isn't much of a talker. If he says he wants a chance, he wants a chance. Dane told me years ago that he thought Jake had a thing for you, but he was too stupid to do anything about it. I can see why you might get hung up on the shifter thing because he was so weird about it after what happened with Naomi. I'm not going to be ridiculous and pretend like you should just believe it will be amazing, but I know you shouldn't try to shut it down because you're scared. If two people ever should be together, it's you and Jake." Shana's words were strong and confident, an antidote to Phoebe's swirling confusion and self-doubt.

Phoebe took a deep breath and met Shana's eyes. "Have I mentioned you're the best friend ever?"

Shana rolled her eyes. "Not always, but I try. As far as friends go, you deserve an award. You've been a rock for me since Callen died and reality as I knew it was turned upside down."

Phoebe felt tears press behind her eyes. Another deep breath, and she thought she could keep it together. Between her raw feelings for Jake and the weeks of topsy-turvy news that had been so devastating for Shana and Catamount, she needed to pull herself together. They had to sort out their next steps while they waited for Dane and Jake to arrive. "Well, that's what friends are for. What now?"

Shana glanced around the parking lot. "Forgot to mention that Dane told me he arranged for two guards to follow us. Some friend who works in private security lives here."

Phoebe groaned. "Seriously? Dane and Jake are going all out with the alpha mode bullshit. I get they're worried with everything's that's happened, but it's damn annoying that they want to keep tabs on us." As soon as she spoke, she realized she'd essentially done the same to Shana by accompanying her out here. She couldn't quite put her finger on why, but somehow Jake's overprotectiveness was annoying her more than she'd have guessed under the circumstances. She could only assume her feelings were gnarled with the uncertainty she felt about what was happening between them.

Shana shrugged. "I'll admit I think we can handle ourselves, but I'll take some backup. We're not exactly on our home turf here."

***

Jake tossed his suitcase in the trunk with Dane's thudding beside his seconds later. He started the car and cranked the heat before stepping back out to help Dane brush the snow off the car. It was December in Montana, and it had snowed the night before with roughly six inches of snow coating the cars in the airport parking lot. They climbed back into the car, doors slamming simultaneously.

Jake leaned his head back and sighed. "Please tell me Shana told you where they're staying," he said, rolling his head to the side to glance at Dane.

Dane chuckled and nodded. "Yup. They booked a

room at a place just down the highway from here."

"Okay, tell me where to go."

Moments later, they were driving down the highway. Jake took in the view as he drove along. Bozeman was situated in the Gallatin Valley, a beautiful valley with views of six stunning mountain ranges. Snow capped the mountain ranges and hillsides. With winter solstice still ahead, winter had a few weeks before its official appearance, but for all intents and purposes, it was winter in Bozeman. The mountains out West felt different than those in the East. In Maine, it felt as if one was part of the nooks and crannies of the mountains. Here, the mountains held themselves at more of a distance, their greater size dominating the landscape. The breadth and spread of the view was immense.

Jake could see why wild mountain lions flourished out here. The logistical realities of more space had afforded them more capacity to elude the press of human expansion that had decimated eastern mountain lions before they evolved the ability to shift. The mere thought of what it would feel like to run wild and free here in lion form rippled under his skin. He had to fight the urge to shift. Shifters hadn't kept themselves safe for centuries by shifting in plain sight.

He glanced at Dane. "Any word from Shana?"

Dane shook his head, lines bracketing his mouth. "Aside from her call earlier, no. She worries me. Ever since she got it in her head that she needed to help with the investigation, she's been brushing me off. She's so devastated about what Callen did, it's like she's trying to make amends for him by somehow fixing this. I know she knows it intellectually, but she's not grasping how far this could go. If only we were dealing with one or two people, or shifters, but my gut tells me we're dealing with far more than that."

Jake had been battling his fear and frustration with Phoebe ever since he'd learned she'd left with Shana yesterday. Unlike Shana, he didn't think she was being buffeted by grief and the array of emotions connected to Callen's betrayal of Catamount shifters and everyone close to him. He understood why she hadn't wanted Shana to go alone, but he somehow wished she'd waited to talk to him first. He didn't want to be angry with her, but he was. Behind that anger laid intense fear. Before he'd finally given into his feelings for her, he would have been worried and scared if she'd taken off like this. He'd have been doing precisely as he was now and chasing after her. Yet, now that he'd experienced the intimacy he'd craved for years with her, he was near out of his mind with worry and fear.

"Jake, you listening?"

He glanced to Dane and back at the highway unrolling in front of him. "Huh?"

Dane shook his head. "You drove past the exit for the hotel. Might want to turn around."

Jake swore and quickly took the next exit and headed back from where they came.

Dane was quiet until they were back on the highway. "I'm guessing you've got Phoebe on the brain. Has she called yet?"

"She left a message. When I tried to call back, it went straight to voice mail."

"Whatever's going on between you two, you're gonna have to play with a level head here."

Jake slanted his eyes to Dane. "No worries about that."

"Maybe you could convince me if you didn't look so pissed off."

"I'm not pissed off. I'm worried. Big difference."

"Whatever. Keep a lid on it," Dane said bluntly.

Following Dane's gesture, Jake exited and swiftly turned into the hotel parking lot Dane pointed out. He parked and turned to Dane. "You don't need to worry. Just like you kept it together with what happened to Chloe, I'll keep it together here. I'm not gonna relax until they're back on a plane to Maine though."

Dane nodded. "You and me both." He paused and glanced around. "I don't see their rental car. Let me call Jon."

Jon Cross was one of Dane's old college friends. Jake knew him in passing, but Dane had gotten to know him when they worked together at a landscaping company. Jon worked in private security and had agreed to monitor Shana and Phoebe. Dane tucked the phone against his shoulder while he spoke to Jon.

"Where? Have you talked to them?" Dane asked, pausing and nodding along to whatever Jon was saying. "What? You're fucking kidding me. We're on our way."

Dane tossed his phone on the dashboard. "Go. They followed Shana and Phoebe to some place for lunch downtown. Shana knew I asked Jon to monitor them, I can't fucking believe she lost them!"

"What? What the hell do you mean?!"

"Just what I said. They went to lunch, went to the restroom, which was out of sight, and that's the last he saw of them. I don't have time to tear him apart like I want, but we're going to find them."

Jake's heart clenched, fear and anger clashing inside. He tore out of the parking lot and back onto the highway. His anger was shoved out of the way with pounding fear. He couldn't stand the thought of Phoebe putting herself in danger like this. He didn't know if she and Shana had purposefully tried to dodge the protection Dane arranged, or if something else had happened. With what he'd pieced together from Callen's online communications, he had multiple contacts in this area. They were interested enough in Catamount shifters to solicit allies within the community and send two shifters their way. Whatever that meant, it didn't bode well for Phoebe's safety. He knew she was bright and savvy—the opposite of a pushover, but she wasn't a shifter. Unlike Shana, if she was physically threatened, she didn't have the ability to shift and attack.

He could hardly bear to consider the thought she could be hurt, but the reality of it loomed much closer than he wanted. His cat strained to get out, but he had to drive and they had to lay low. He tightened the reins on his control and drove as fast as he could.

Chapter 9

"Shana," Phoebe whispered fiercely.

"Hang on, I'm trying to see where they are."

Phoebe sighed and leaned against the cabin. They were in the foothills of the mountains outside of Bozeman. Shana was convinced she'd seen Paul, the patient they'd thought to be a shifter at the hospital. She'd started to argue with Phoebe when Phoebe had pointed out they should wait for Jake and Dane. After waiting far too long for Shana to return from the bathroom at lunch, Phoebe found her sneaking out the back of the restaurant. Resigned, Phoebe had gone with her and followed Paul out here. They'd stationed themselves at what appeared to be a hunting cabin on the outskirts of the forest and were watching a cluster of people in a small valley nearby.

Phoebe wondered where Jake and Dane were and how pissed off they were at this point. A part of her knew she needed to be the voice of reason with Shana, while another part of her figured they should act on whatever they found. She was savvy enough to take care of herself out here and would retreat if needed. Her main concern was

Shana. She was quickly coming to realize she hadn't grasped the depth of Shana's drive to handle this. Shana wasn't being reasonable, and Phoebe feared she'd shift and bolt. If that happened, Phoebe wouldn't be able to stop her.

Shana suddenly came back around the corner of the cabin, immediately coming to Phoebe's side and resting against the cabin wall. She handed over the binoculars she'd been using. "Well, they're definitely shifters."

"They are?"

Shana nodded. "Just watched two of the men, Paul included, shift. I don't think all of them are though. It's hard to tell this far away, but they don't all have the look."

Phoebe nodded. Tension was knotted so tight in her gut, she didn't know what to do. Between worrying about Shana and aware that they were far from home in a potentially risky situation, her anxiety ran high. "Shana, I think we need to get back to the hotel and call Dane and Jake."

Shana glanced at her and then away. "I know. I just wanted to see if we could figure out where Paul was going, and we did. I'm not stupid enough to take them on myself. Let's go."

Phoebe was so relieved, she hugged Shana quickly. When she pulled away, she saw the lingering sadness in Shana's eyes, but her eyes had lost the touch of recklessness she'd seen earlier. "Come on. Let's go." Looping her arm through Shana's, they walked quickly back to the rental car parked at the gravel lot near the trailhead that led to the cabin they'd found.

As they drove back to the hotel, Phoebe considered what she'd say to Jake when she saw him. By the time they arrived, she'd come to no conclusions. Shana had called Dane on the way, and he and Jake were waiting in the parking lot when they pulled in.

When she climbed out of the car and saw Jake lounging against the car, she couldn't stop herself from running to him. Even though his gaze could have burned a hole through her, he looked so angry, his arms reflexively went around her when she raced up and threw her arms around him. She tucked her head against his shoulder and held on. She was confused, scared and tired, but being in his arms was like coming home. She knew she had to sort out how she was going to handle whatever this was, but for now, she just needed to know he was here.

His strong arms held her until she finally lifted her head. When she met his eyes, he slowly let her slide down his body. His mouth kicked up at the corner in a rueful grin. "I was plenty pissed off and scared, but I get why you came with Shana."

She nodded. "I tried to call you…"

Dane cleared his throat. "Sorry to interrupt, but it's fucking freezing out here. Let's get inside. You two lovebirds might not notice, but the rest of us do," he said wryly.

Phoebe glanced over at Dane and then met Shana's eyes, a blush racing up her neck and face. "Right. Let's get inside."

Shana rolled her eyes and started walking toward the hotel lobby. As she did, she glanced over her shoulder at Jake. "I told Phoebe it's about damn time."

Jake chuckled and hooked his arm around Phoebe's waist, walking in stride with her.

***

Hours later, they'd filled Jake and Dane in on their afternoon escapade and were sitting at the small round table in their hotel suite looking at a map of the area. They'd had to put up with a lecture from Dane and Jake, but all in all, they'd kept it civil thus far. Phoebe sensed Jake had quite a bit more to share about how he felt about her taking off like that, but he was holding back for now.

Dane penciled in the area where Shana had seen the shifters and had Jake pull up his data from the various ISP addresses he'd identified. Phoebe was wired and tired at the same time. She sat beside Jake, her legs in his lap. He absently stroked one leg with his palm, the heat of it sifting through her leggings like a drug. She'd thought she'd be more self-conscious being like this with him in front of their friends, but strangely she wasn't. She figured she might find it more difficult in Catamount where the change in their relationship would be obvious to all. Somehow, here in another place so removed from home, she found it easier to relax and accept the way they were.

A low charge hummed between them at all times. They'd gone out to dinner with Dane and Shana, and she'd managed to behave appropriately, but just barely. Jake wasn't making it any easier with his hands on her someway, somewhere, somehow no matter where they were. Just now, his thumb stroked into the crease at the top of her thigh, coasting so close to the center of her desire that she had to force herself to hold her hips still. Heat pooled in her belly, liquid need thrumming through her.

"So between what you two discovered today and Jake's data, we can pinpoint a circle of locations for those ISP addresses right around where you saw them today," Dane said, his words breaking through the fog of desire Phoebe was drifting in.

Jake was nodding along. "Maybe we should pay a visit to Hayden Thorne."

Dane nodded. "I'm thinking that's where we start tomorrow."

"Who's that?" Shana asked.

"He's one of the people Callen emailed with frequently. He works for the Feds in Fish & Wildlife. From what I can gather, he's not part of the smuggling network, but we're not sure. Either way, he's official, so we can safely visit him at his office and see what we think."

"Are you insane?" Phoebe asked, sitting up straighter in her chair, snapped out of her dazed state. "You can't throw yourself in the path of the Feds. Catamount shifters don't need someone like that nosing around."

Shana nodded emphatically. "I'm with Phoebe on this one. Let's not make things worse."

Jake met Phoebe's eyes, his bright blue gaze steady. "Callen already put Catamount in his radar. If he's one of the bad guys, he's already on to us. From what I read of his emails, he was not one of the contacts Callen met out here."

Phoebe glanced to Shana who pursed her lips and shrugged. Phoebe had had it drummed into her that shifters had only managed to survive by keeping their secrets safe. Her connections to Catamount shifters ran deep, so she'd held the secret of their existence close and didn't like the idea of putting them in the path of the government.

Dane nodded to Jake. "He's right. If this guy's on the wrong side, he already knows where Callen lived and had plenty of leads to follow. Us showing up won't change that, but it might give us some ideas."

Phoebe met Jake's eyes again, which were steady and determined. She shrugged. "Fine, but you guys better be careful."

Dane's gaze bounced between her and Shana. "We'll be careful, but after what you two pulled, you're not exactly on high ground."

Phoebe fought the urge to point out she'd only followed Shana out here to try to make sure she was safe. Much as she wanted to argue the point, she didn't want to turn the focus on Shana. Shana might be behaving a bit recklessly right now, but she'd been through so much. Phoebe understood Shana was driven by the pain and grief behind Callen's death and betrayal. Shana huffed and rolled her eyes. "Nothing happened, so there's no need to lecture us anymore."

Jake swung to Shana, his eyes sobering. "You're damn lucky nothing happened. It was bad enough you dragged Phoebe into this with you…"

Shana cut him off. "I didn't drag Phoebe anywhere! She…"

Jake's hand slashed through the air. "I know damn well Phoebe makes her own decisions, but I also know you're the one that came up with this bright idea. I get why you'd want to help with this after what Callen did. But please stop and think. Chloe getting kidnapped was enough. You're a shifter and Phoebe's not. If something happened and you needed to shift to fight, run, or hide, you can. Phoebe doesn't have that option. I'm not pissed, but I will be if you keep trying to downplay everything." Jake's words were low and taut.

Phoebe jumped when his hand tightened on her leg. Jake immediately turned to her, his gaze softening. He loosened his palm and stroked it slowly up and down her leg. Phoebe was awash in emotion. Intellectually, she thought she should be annoyed at Jake's protectiveness, but it thrilled her. In the many years they'd been friends, he'd tended to treat her as if she was invincible. It was beyond nice to have him concerned for her safety. And if he didn't stop driving her mad with his hand absently wandering up and down her legs, she might embarrass them both. She took a breath and looked around the table.

Shana stared at the armrest of her chair and traced the curved edge with her fingertip. She sighed and looked up. "All right, I didn't think of it that way." She glanced to Phoebe and bit her lip. "Thanks for coming with me. I know you did it because you wanted to make sure I'd be okay. Jake's right though." Turning her gaze to Jake, Shana lifted her chin. "I still say we can take care of ourselves, but you have a point."

Dane shook his head and chuckled. "Never thought I'd see the day you admitted Jake might be right. You know if you're saying he's right, it means I'm right too, right?"

Shana tossed a balled up napkin at him from the debris of their after dinner snacking. "Bask in your moment because it won't happen again anytime soon."

Conversation moved on to planning the next few days. Phoebe lost focus entirely, her attention occupied by Jake's nearness—the absentminded teases of his palm stroking her leg, his thumb softly coasting across the nub of her desire. The table masked his motions. She all but forgot Dane and Shana were in the room with them. At one point, she closed her eyes, savoring the sensations teeming through her body.

Eventually, Shana retired to her room off the suite, and Dane claimed he'd take the couch. When Dane went out to the car to get something, Jake stood swiftly, lifting her in his arms and striding into the other bedroom, kicking the door shut behind them. In one smooth motion, he knelt on the bed and stretched her out underneath him, his full length coming atop her with her wrists pinned above her head by one of his hands.

Her pulse quickened when his eyes met hers, burning into her. She was spun tight inside from his careless teasing for the last hour or so. He whispered her name, his voice rough and raw, before he claimed her lips. His kiss was fierce. She was instantly engulfed in the heat of the moment—hot, needy, liquid want poured through her. Her tongue tangled with his. She was desperate to get closer. He shifted over her, arching his hips into hers, the hot, hard evidence of his arousal pressing against her own. She gasped into his mouth. He pulled back, his blue gaze boring into her.

"Don't scare me like that again."

Though his words could have been perceived as an order, they felt like an endearment. She shook her head. "I won't. I…"

"No need to explain. I know exactly why you went with Shana. That's the kind of friend you are. But I can't take it if something happens to you." His voice broke, and he took a gulp of air. Suddenly, he pushed off of her. He moved with ruthless efficiency. In a flash, her clothes were tugged off and his tossed aside. The room was cool, her skin pebbling. The heat of his body surrounded her. This time when he stretched over her, she gasped at the feel of his heated skin against hers. He stroked a hand roughly through her hair. Holding still for a moment, he met her eyes, his gaze hot and electric. Cupping her cheek, he brought his lips to hers again, his thumb coasting over her pulse as he stroked down her neck, traced the line of her collarbone and dipped to curl around her breast.

The low charge that hummed within her whenever he was near exploded, molten heat erupting in her center and spiraling outward. She felt his touch everywhere at once. His lips teasing her ear and blazing a trail down her neck. His fingers rolling her nipples between them, softly tugging and nipping. Kisses dusted all over her body, his hands soft and hard at once, the roughened skin driving her mad. The tip of his cock at her entrance, making her ache for him to be inside of her.

She couldn't get close enough, her hands skating over his hard, muscled body, scoring his back with her nails. When he reached for the condom he'd tossed on the nightstand, she grabbed his arm. "There's no need. I'm on the pill."

Jake froze, his head turning slowly to her. "Phoebe…"

She suddenly felt self-conscious. She simply wanted to be as close to him as she could, no barriers. And there really was no need. Despite her discomfort, she'd started this, so she had to see it through. "Jake, there's no point to it. I'm on the pill, and I can barely remember the last time I had sex before you. I'm clean. I know you are too. If you insist…"

His lips curled in heated smile before he claimed her mouth again. Though she couldn't have fathomed it, he proceeded to notch the heat between them higher and higher. His touch became rougher, less measured. She writhed and flexed underneath him, desperate to feel him inside of her. His lips grazed down her neck again. He tugged her hands up, pinning them above her head. When she arched into him, his lips closed around a nipple, his teeth nipping, the soft bite drawing a cry from her.

"Jake…please…"

He murmured a reply against her breast and lifted his head. She lost herself in his dark blue gaze as he slowly shifted his hips, the tip of his cock teasing her entrance, drenched with want. Her breath came in ragged gasps as he teased her beyond sanity. When she spoke his name again, he surged inside, to the hilt, in one swift move. The pressure built higher and higher inside of her. He stroked into and out of her completely each time, stretching and filling her over and over again. Tremors spiraled outward from her center until she shattered, her climax wrenching through her. He swallowed her cries in his mouth, gasping into hers as he surged into her one last time, shuddering against her. His mouth stilled and pulled away. He rested his forehead against hers. Their ragged breathing filled the room and slowed in unison. They were still until Jake slowly released his grip on her wrists and stroked his hand down her side, tracing her curves.

"You're getting cold," he murmured before slowly pulling out of her and rolling to the side to tug the covers out from under them. In seconds, she was curled in his arms under the comforter, his warmth filtering through her.

Chapter 10

Jake glanced around as he and Dane walked up to Hayden Thorne's office. The office building sat against the foothills of the mountains encircling Bozeman. A fresh dusting of snow had fallen during the night. A soft mist hung in the cold air as the sun crested above the mountains, glittering the landscape where it struck sparks on the snow. He kicked his boots against the threshold to knock the clinging snow off as they stepped inside. Dane followed suit. The office was quiet and the reception desk empty. Dane tapped the bell that sat on the desk.

A moment passed and then one of the office doors opened, a man leaning his head through the door. "Good morning, can I help you?"

Jake nodded. "We're looking for Hayden Thorne."

The man in question arched a brow and stepped out of his office. Jake knew without a doubt he was a shifter. He was tall and lanky, his body giving off a sense of coiled energy, an underlying thread of leashed power. He had golden brown hair and caramel eyes, a feline cast to his features. He glanced between Jake and Dane before stepping forward to offer his hand. “Well, that would be me.” He paused and nodded to the empty reception desk. “Our receptionist is out sick today, so I hope you didn’t wait too long.”

After quickly introducing themselves, Dane commented, “If now’s not a good time, we can come back later.”

Hayden shook his head. “Now’s as good a time as any. Come on in.” He gestured for them to sit at a table in his office and closed the door before joining them. “What can I do for you?”

Jake’s gut reinforced his perception from the many emails he read from Hayden to Callen that Hayden was not a bad guy, so he decided to get right to the point. “Does the name Callen Peyton sound familiar?”

Hayden’s gaze sharpened. He nodded slowly. “Sure does. How is it that you know Callen?”

“Callen’s dead,” Dane said flatly.

Jake cut in. “I found your name in some emails between you and Callen. We have reason to believe he got involved with some shady characters out here before he died. I’ll be honest, I’m not sure if we’re crazy to talk to you, seeing as you work for the Feds, but Callen opened up a can of worms before he died. We need to find out more about what he was doing out here and what you might know.”

Hayden leaned back in his chair, flipping a pen between his fingers. “And how is it you think I can help?”

Jake leaned forward, anger flashing through him. They didn’t have time for vague communication. He knew damn well Hayden had some idea of what was going on. “Callen was in regular communication with you about mountain lion shifters out here. Since he died, we’ve had two shifters show up from out of nowhere and a kidnapping. We don't have time to drag this out. Either you help us out, or we'll keep investigating on our own. If you think for a second I would hesitate to make your involvement public, think again."

Hayden held Jake's gaze, appearing unruffled by Jake's comment. A weighted silence hung in the room before Hayden set the pen down and leaned forward, resting his elbows on the table. "I suppose we're all going to have to take a leap of faith here. I've heard both of your names and followed the local news in Maine about the kidnapping. Based on your roles in that situation and my gut, I'm going to assume we can trust each other."

Jake held his silence, but relief washed through him. He'd had his doubts about coming here to meet with Hayden. Catamount shifters definitely didn't need a spotlight from the Federal Fish & Wildlife shining on them. But Callen had already put them in its glare in his communications with Hayden. Jake had hoped against hope they might catch a break. Hayden's cooperation was a start.

Hayden continued. "Callen started emailing me over a year ago. I knew right off he was scenting out if there were mountain lion shifters out here. I didn't realize until later on that he'd linked up with a bad crowd of shifters. I've been investigating some of the shifters Callen fell in with over the last few years. I'm guessing you're after the same thing I am—to find out who's involved and who holds the power."

Dane caught Jake's gaze and nodded. "You guessed right," he said, addressing his comment to Jake before turning to Hayden. "We knew something wasn't right when Callen died. We knew he was trying to confirm if there were shifters out here, but it made absolutely no sense that he was traveling back East in lion form. Jake works in computers and coding, along with online forensic investigations. As soon as he started sifting through Callen's email accounts, he discovered Callen had been trying to set a price on using Catamount shifters for drug smuggling."

Jake picked up the thread here. "I came across his emails with you, but none of the smuggling details were mentioned. Later on, if I had to guess, you seemed to be trying to warn him away from some of the guys he connected with."

Hayden nodded firmly. "Once I put the pieces together, I tried to head him off. But you know how that goes. I didn't want to give too much away, and it became clear he was going to do what he wanted. I backed off after that, only staying in touch to track when he came out here." Hayden paused, a muscle in his jaw ticking. "So, am I to understand you all didn't know anything about what he was doing until after he died?"

Dane ran a hand through his hair and shook his head with a sigh. "Not a damn thing. He was my brother-in-law. My sister, his wife, had no clue. She's devastated in more ways than one since she found out what he was doing. After Chloe was kidnapped, the lid blew off. Callen's brother, Randall, was one of the kidnappers. By the way, Chloe's my fiancée. They told her they needed her for leverage with me. We haven't gotten much else from them, but they'll be sitting tight in jail for now. Any ideas on that?"

Hayden shrugged. "If I had to guess, I'd say they knew you were a leader in the community. Since Callen died, they probably wanted to persuade you to either support their smuggling operation, or ignore it. I'd love to tell you I knew where this giant mess started. But all I know is a few years ago rumors started swirling around here that shifters were getting paid to smuggle drugs. So far, I've only been able to link it to individuals. Whoever's running this show is not in this area. Until they made contact with Callen, far as I could sniff out, the smuggling was limited to the West from Montana down to New Mexico. The big money comes from smuggling from Mexico into the United States. With so many mountain lions out here, it's easy for shifters to move freely when they are in lion form as long as they steer mostly clear of urban areas. I'd like to say I was surprised they wanted to work out East, but it's about money. If they can start funneling the drugs to the East Coast, that's a huge market. I didn't think Callen would be stupid enough to fall for it. Mountain lions have been considered extinct out East for a long damn time. You can't move freely. I don't know how you manage it."

Jake sat back with a sigh. Hayden was confirming his suspicions. He'd hoped Hayden would have more information about who might be behind this. "Any ideas on who started this?"

"Not much to go on. I don't think it started here though. I can point you to a few local shifters who I know to be involved, but their involvement is what Callen's was. I've been investigating this since I heard about it, but it's not exactly easy. You might think I'm crazy to be working for the Feds, but I've had this job for years. Being a shifter in this role means I've got my ear to the ground about any rumors about shifters. We don't have to worry as much as you do out East, but the last thing we need is for people to find out shifters truly exist. Myth works in our favor."

Dane glanced to Jake. "Mind giving us a few names for the locals involved?"

"Not at all. I'm glad to know you're working on this too. Maybe between us, we can find the source. Ever since Callen died and then I saw the news about the kidnapping in Catamount, I wondered if anyone would show up out here."

Jake leaned back in his chair. Tension knotted his shoulders, and he rolled his head around to ease it. "We meant to get out here eventually, but circumstances forced our hand sooner."

At Hayden's arched brow, Jake and Dane quickly summarized the events in Catamount and Shana and Phoebe's unexpected journey. When Dane mentioned the shifters Shana and Phoebe had seen yesterday, Hayden swore. "The last thing they need to be doing is heading out in the foothills around here. I don't know about your numbers back East, but easily half the mountain lions you might encounter out here are shifters. The area they found happens to be the camp of one of the local guys who's been smuggling."

Anger tightened its coil inside Jake. He couldn't think about Phoebe without being afraid of what could have happened. Right now, he just wanted to march her to the airport and get her back to Catamount. Reason reminded him that Chloe hadn't been safe in Catamount, so he couldn't assume Phoebe would be safe there either. All he knew was he couldn't bear to think of her at risk.

***

Phoebe took a sip of coffee and glanced around the diner where she and Shana had come for a late breakfast. She'd woken in the early hours of the morning with Jake spooned behind her. The gray light of dawn filtered through the curtains. The feel of his heartbeat against her back had sent desire curling through her veins. A sharp knock at their door had interrupted the moment. Jake had dropped a soft kiss on the back of her neck before rolling out of bed. He'd called to Dane that they'd be out shortly and proceeded to drive her wild inside of five minutes.

He departed after she was all but limp, leaning against the shower wall, shudders reverberating through her. The recollection made her flush. She shook her head, forcing her mind back to the moment.

"So, you and Jake?" Shana asked, a teasing glint in her eyes.

Phoebe nodded, her flush returning. "Yeah. I, uh, didn't really expect it. But things seem to be happening. I'm not sure what it means in the long run." She paused and considered what to say. Shana was her closest friend, yet Phoebe had held the secret of her feelings for Jake close because she'd never thought it would amount to anything. She took a breath to get to the other side of her nerves. "Honestly, if I let myself think about it much, I go a little crazy." She stopped there, not ready to say aloud what her heart knew. Things had already progressed too far, too fast with Jake. They'd blown past the point where they could ever return to being just friends. She didn't know how her heart would survive if it didn't work out. Her initial fears about losing their friendship seemed quaint and simple now. Now, she feared her heart would be shattered.

Shana looked at her for a long moment, her blue-gray eyes soft and warm. "He loves you, you know."

Shana's words slammed into her center, sending butterflies up in a swirl inside. "You think so?"

Shana nodded slowly. "I've always thought he loved you for years, just like I thought you loved him. I didn't say anything about it because he was stuck on not dating any woman who wasn't a shifter, and I figured you didn't want to rock the boat. I always meant to eventually give him a good shake, but he seems to have finally come to his senses on his own."

"Was it that obvious?" Hope beat like a drum in her heart. To hear Shana say she thought Jake always loved her was a thread she grabbed and held onto, hoping it would lead her to what her heart so desperately wanted to believe.

"If you mean how you felt about him, it wasn't too obvious. I had a hunch because I know you so well. To anyone else, it probably wasn't so obvious. As for Jake, Dane thought it was obvious and he knows Jake better than anyone."

Phoebe added a dash of cream to her coffee, watching the swirl as she stirred it in. "I'm trying not to worry, but it's hard. I love him. I managed to keep it together all this time. If this blows up, I'm not so sure I can handle it." Her breath caught, her throat was tight. She met Shana's gaze. "On the one hand, this is what I wanted for so long, I almost can't believe it. On the other, I'm in too deep already. If this doesn't work out, I'll lose everything I had with him because I can't go back to being his friend."

Shana tilted her head and sighed. "How about you focus on what's happening instead of what's not happening?"

Phoebe twirled an errant curl around her finger and echoed Shana's sigh. "I'll try."

Shana reached over and squeezed her hand. "With everything I've had to come to terms with lately, I've become a big fan of focusing on the moment. I could spend all day obsessing over memories, wondering how I could have missed what Callen was doing, but it doesn't change a damn thing." A tear tipped over Shana's lashes, and she swiftly wiped it away.

"Shana, I'm so sorry. I wish…"

Shana shook her head. "I know you want to fix it, to make it all better. You've been the best friend ever through all of this just by being there. I'm hanging in there. I know I shouldn't have pressured you to come with me out here, but I'm damn glad you did."

Phoebe's eyes filled with tears, so sad for what Shana was going through and wishing she could find a way to ease her grief. Their waitress arrived at that moment, hesitating when she caught their expressions. She started to back away when Shana shook her head. "Oh, don't you worry. Food will help," she said with a wry grin.

After their waitress served them and refilled their coffee, Shana met Phoebe's eyes, lifting her coffee mug up in a toast. "To friends and second chances."

Phoebe clinked her mug against Shana's and dug into her pancakes. As their conversation moved onto lighter matters, Jake and Dane arrived with an unfamiliar man in tow. In short order, they were seated at the booth and had ordered breakfast. Hayden introduced himself. Conversation stayed superficial though Jake and Dane had both assured them that Hayden was on the safe side. As they ate, Jake's leg pressed against hers in the crowded booth. It didn't matter that only hours earlier she'd been tangled up with him, she wanted him with every breath and every beat of her heart.

Chapter 11

Phoebe walked alongside Shana in downtown Bozeman. Jake and Dane had headed back to another meeting with Hayden to review data Jake had compiled. Phoebe and Shana headed downtown for the superficial purpose of shopping, while also following up on some tips Hayden offered about a few areas shifters frequented. Dane and Jake had grudgingly agreed after Hayden assured them that he considered the area safe due to its density. Downtown Bozeman included a historical district filled with art galleries, shopping and restaurants. After Jake and Dane had shared that Hayden estimated half of the mountain lion population out here were shifters, Phoebe found herself constantly assessing everyone they encountered. Though Catamount was heavily populated with shifters, their existence back East was much more prescribed. Mountain lions had healthy populations throughout much of the West. It was strange to consider shifters had such a presence here. Within the context of recent events, this worried Phoebe. She didn't know whom she could trust beyond her small circle of friends.

Shana hooked her hand in Phoebe's elbow and tugged her into another art gallery. "We have to bring something home for Roxanne and Lily."

Roxanne was a good friend of both of theirs, along with Lily who was Jake's younger sister. Phoebe glanced around the gallery, which was filled with a mix of pottery, jewelry, metal sculptures and watercolors. Shana gestured to where she was headed while Phoebe moved to look through the pottery selection. The gallery was busy with a low hum of conversation and soft music in the background. She found a pair of mugs she thought Roxanne would like when she thought she heard someone say her name. When she looked around, she couldn't find anyone looking in her direction. She headed toward where she'd last seen Shana, but couldn't find her. Unease snaked up her spine. She spent the next few minutes circling the gallery. Shana was nowhere to be found. She finally asked a salesperson if they'd seen Shana, providing a brief description of her.

The woman gave her an odd look and slowly nodded. "Yeah, there was a woman here who looked like that. She left with a man. I thought they were together. He had her by the arm. Is everything okay?" she asked, her eyes widening.

Fear bolted through Phoebe, knotting in her belly. "Are you sure she left?"

"I'm only sure a woman who looked like the one you described left. If that's her, yes, she left."

"Oh my God! Did you recognize the man with her?"

The woman's eyes were wide with fear at this point. She shook her head rapidly. "I'm sorry. I didn't know she wasn't with him. Let me call the police for you." She stepped to the counter and called.

Phoebe fumbled in her purse, tapping on Shana's

number immediately. To her relief, Shana answered. "It's me," she whispered.

"Where are you?" Phoebe asked, stepping out of the way of some customers by the counter.

"Across the street at a little café. One of the men I saw yesterday when we were in the woods came up and asked me if we could talk. I told him I'd only meet in public. Don't freak out, I'm in plain sight. He went to order something at the counter. I was just about to call you."

Phoebe's heart didn't slow, but she was able to catch her breath. She was furious with Shana. Every time she thought Shana's recklessness was waning, she went and did something like this. Phoebe glanced up and gestured at the saleswoman, pointing to her phone and giving a thumbs up. "I'm coming over now. Don't hang up. I want you on the line with me until I get there."

She strode briskly over to the saleswoman, tilting the phone away. "I'm on the line with my friend. No need to call the police, but thank you for your help." At the woman's nod and smile, Phoebe turned and raced outside, asking Shana every few seconds if she was still there. When she saw the small café across the street, she jogged over and walked inside.

Shana sat at a small table by herself. She waved once she saw Phoebe. The line went dead in Phoebe's ear when Shana tucked her phone in her pocket. Phoebe slipped into the chair beside Shana.

"Where's the guy you followed over here?" Phoebe asked immediately.

Shana shrugged. "After he asked if I wanted to talk, all he said was we should be careful. He left after he got a coffee. I was about to call you when you called me. I figured you'd be about to freak out. Aside from the fact that he pissed me off when he grabbed my arm, I figured I'd be safe because we were in the middle of so many people."

Phoebe forced herself to breathe slowly. "Did you forget Chloe was kidnapped in in the middle of downtown Catamount?"

Shana didn't flinch though Phoebe knew her tone was sharp. "No. I didn't forget. It might have been the middle of Catamount, but it was late afternoon when not many people were around. We were in a crowd over there. I get that you're pissed, but I figured I might as well see what he had to say. Not much though."

Phoebe took another breath, her pulse finally slowing down. The fear that had knotted in her belly loosened. She held her words back. Part of her wanted to lecture Shana, but she wasn't Shana's best friend for nothing. She knew Shana well enough to know a lecture would only result in Shana completely ignoring her. At the moment, Shana was safe and that was all that mattered.

"Did he happen to mention his name?"

Shana shook her head. "It's weird. I kinda think he wanted to make sure we were okay. Or if he meant to say something else, he changed his mind." She paused and glanced around. "Do you want to get something to eat while we're here?"

Phoebe took another breath. Her initial thought was to say no, but she was starving. "Why not? I'm calling Jake though."

Shana nodded quickly. "I'm not being stupid. I already texted Dane. He wants us to meet them back at the hotel."

***

A mountain lion raced into the foothills behind Hayden's office. Jake paused as they walked across the parking lot. His lion rippled under the surface of his skin.

He turned to Dane who walked beside him. "See that?"

Dane nodded tightly. "I'd like to follow, but I'm thinking we need to touch base with Hayden."

Jake resumed walking, striding quickly to the building. Hayden called out for them to come in as soon as they stepped inside.

Jake didn't bother with the preliminaries. "Was that a shifter behind the building?"

Hayden glanced up from his computer. "What?" he asked sharply.

"We just saw a mountain lion behind the building run into the woods," Dane replied.

Hayden stood and walked to the window that faced the woods behind his office. "Those tracks there?" He pointed to fresh tracks leading into the woods. The mountain lion was well out of sight.

"That's right where it went. What are the chances that was a wild cat and not a shifter?" Jake asked.

Hayden shook his head and turned back to them. "Not good. Though there's a healthy population of wild mountain lions out here, they stay away from town. I can never say for sure unless I see them myself, but lions you see near populated areas are most likely shifters. I can recognize most of the locals because I'm one of them." He strode to the coffee maker in the corner. "Coffee?"

Hayden quickly poured three cups when Jake and Dane nodded in unison and then gestured for them to sit at the table. Jake had to fight the urge to bolt and shift. The lion in him wanted to follow the mountain lion he'd just witnessed. He had to keep a tight rein on the impulse. He was getting damn tired of worrying about who was who and what was what. After Shana's brief encounter yesterday where she was warned that they should be careful, the only reason he hadn't forced Phoebe onto a plane was she'd flat out refused. They'd already filled Hayden in on that, along with Shana's description of the man who'd warned her. Hayden's guess was he was one of the locals connected with the shifters who smuggled, but from what Hayden knew, he'd yet to get involved himself.

As they settled in to review what Hayden had gathered in the years he'd been investigating, the door to Hayden's office flew open. Hayden appeared to recognize the man, standing abruptly. The man shifted and leapt toward Hayden. In a flash, Jake shifted along with Dane and Hayden. With a snarl, the unfamiliar shifter swiped at Hayden. In the blur that followed, Jake toppled Hayden's table over, leaping across it to land on the back of the unfamiliar shifter, knocking him to the ground. They cornered him before he slipped underneath Dane and crashed through the window, glass shattering in his wake. In rapid succession, they followed him through the window, racing into the woods behind the office.

Jake had been keeping such a tight, controlled leash on his lion side that the exhilaration of letting loose barreled through him. He raced ahead of Dane and Hayden, primal anger pounding as he chased after the shifter. They threaded through trees as they galloped deeper into the woods, making their way into the foothills. Hayden pulled alongside and thrust his head to one side. When Jake ignored him and kept following the other lion, Hayden growled and bumped his shoulder against Jake. Reluctantly, Jake slowed and eyed Hayden. In lion form, Hayden was roughly equal to him and Dane in size though his build was heavier. When Hayden met his eyes, he tossed his head to the side again and began to move in that direction, pulling them off the trail of the other lion.

Jake looked forward through the trees, the other lion still in clear sight. He gathered his haunches and leapt away from Hayden again, only to have Dane race past him and stop abruptly in front of him, roaring at him. Snow kicked up in a swirl around them. Hayden circled back, pausing beside Dane. Both stared at Jake. Fury pulsed through Jake's veins, but he forced himself to think. Hayden clearly had a reason for nudging them in another direction. Much as Jake wanted to race after the other lion, he didn't know these woods and knew the other lion might be leading them into a trap. With a soft snarl, he pawed at the ground, but held still. Hayden swished his tail as he turned in front and began to trot slowly away. Dane waited until Jake began to follow Hayden.

The terrain became steeper and rockier. Not much later, they crested a small rise. Hayden came to a stop. A small valley lay in view from their vantage point. A cluster of homes was on the opposite side of the valley. Humans milled about in an open area, along with a few mountain lions. From their viewpoint, they could shield themselves behind some boulders. Once they were shielded, Hayden shifted back into human form. Jake and Dane followed. Though it was freezing and they were bare, their clothes discarded on the floor of Hayden's office, the cold didn't touch them. Shifting created so much heat that it would be a good while before they felt the cold.

Hayden met Jake's eyes. "I didn't want you ending up there," he said, gesturing toward the valley. "I don't doubt the two of can hold your own in a fight, but it's a good bet everyone you see there is a shifter. The shifter who showed up in my office is Paul Malone's brother, Neal Malone. Like I said, Paul's your guy from the hospital. He's in deep with the smuggling crew, along with his brother. There's no sense in us taking a fight to them on their territory. Callen's death has shaken things up. I think they're worried about exposure and want to limit their losses. We need to target who we can away from the crowd. I haven't seen Paul since he took off a few weeks ago. Aside from when Shana saw him the other day when she and Phoebe were out scouting, he's been laying low. I'd like to knock him out of circulation and see what we can get out of him. For now, let's get the hell out of here. As soon as I saw where Neal was taking us, I figured he was hoping to trap us there."

Jake had to fight to keep himself from taking off again. He glanced at Dane and saw frustration mirrored in his eyes. He looked back to Hayden. "Any ideas where we can find Paul?"

"I have some ideas. Let's get going and we'll head back out another time."

Hayden didn't wait for their reply and shifted again. Jake and Dane followed and retraced their path, this time at a slower pace.

Chapter 12

Phoebe sat on the couch in their hotel suite, idly flipping through channels. She and Shana were waiting for Jake and Dane. He'd texted earlier to say they'd be back soon. The door to their suite opened and Jake walked in with Dane right behind him. His blue eyes locked on hers as soon as he stepped into the room. Energy came off of him in waves. Their clothing was torn in places. Jake offered a perfunctory nod and hello to Shana.

"Mind if we take a few minutes?" Jake asked, his gaze breaking from Phoebe's to bounce between Shana and Dane. Dane's mouth quirked as he nodded. Shana merely shrugged. Jake grabbed Phoebe's hand as he strode toward her, pulling her up swiftly. The second the door closed on their room, he tugged her to him, kissing her fiercely and tearing at her clothes.

Phoebe pulled back, pressing her hand on his chest to hold him still. His heart pounded against her palm. His eyes held hers, burning her with his gaze. "What happened?" She slid her hand across his chest, curling over his shoulder and down his arm. She paused over a tear in his sleeve and arched a brow.

He closed his eyes, his breath labored. "We had to shift when a guy showed up at Hayden's office and shifted right there. No harm done though, you don't need to worry."

"Jake…"

Her words were swallowed in his kiss. He lifted her in his arms and covered the distance to the bathroom in two long strides. He shouldered through the door and took her mouth in another bruising kiss. She tumbled into the vortex of heat swirling between them. Never breaking contact from her lips, Jake eased her onto the small counter and reached inside the shower with one hand to turn it on. Steam filled the room in seconds. Clothes were torn off and left on the floor. He nudged the soft light on above the shower.

She wrapped her legs around his waist, glorying in the feel of his hard muscled body under her hands. His touch was everywhere at once and she couldn't get enough. He lifted her high against his body, the center of her resting against his shaft—hot and hard against her soft, slick folds. Steam enveloped them when he stepped into the shower. Hot water rained down upon them as he slowly loosened his hold and she slid down his body. Without pause, she kept moving down, her hands coasting down his chest, across his rock hard abs, and down his thighs. His breath hissed through his teeth when she curled her hand around his cock.

She glanced up through the steam and caught his eyes, his dark blue gaze intent on her. Desire snaked around them. Holding his eyes, she leaned forward and slowly stroked up and down his cock with her tongue. He groaned and his head fell back. She took him in her mouth, to the hilt, and then drew back slowly. Establishing a steady rhythm, desire sizzled through her as she toyed and teased with him. After a deep stroke, Jake growled her name and moved swiftly, tugging her up and turning her to face the shower wall.

The tile was cool under her palms. His strong palm stroked down her back, sliding through the water. He nudged into her folds, but held still as tension drew tight inside of her. His lips landed on her spine and trailed upward in a dizzying path of kisses. When he reached her neck, he bit softly just as he thrust inside of her. She gasped as he filled her. Without his hands holding her hips, she'd have fallen. Enveloped in sensation, her focus centered on the slow pull and slide of his shaft inside her channel. Twisting heat built within her until she was spun tight. Another nip on her neck and she shattered, unwinding into wave after wave of her climax. He growled her name again and then arched back, pounding into her as he found his own release.

Phoebe felt the hot water coasting over her skin and slowly slid her palms up the tile. Jake stepped away from her though his hand remained curled on her hip even as she turned to face him. His golden brown hair stood in wet spikes, his lashes glistening. He met her eyes, a wicked smile curling the corner of his mouth. Without a word, his hand fell away and he grabbed the soap, quickly soaping her and then himself. He pulled her close to rinse the soap off, the steaming water sluicing over them as he held her in his arms.

Moments later, he wrapped her in a towel and stood watching her while she briskly rubbed her hair with another towel. She glanced up to find him leaning against the doorframe, arms crossed with a bemused expression.

"That was more than a few minutes," she said, in reference to his comment to Dane and Shana.

Jake shrugged. "Don't care."

She set the towel down and ran her fingers through her damp curls. She walked past him into the bedroom, collecting their scattered clothing as she did. Holding up his torn shirt, she turned back to him.

"What happened this afternoon?"

"Like I said, some guy showed up at Hayden's office and shifted. He went after Hayden and when we shifted and fought back, he took off into the woods. We followed, but Hayden made me back off. The guy was headed straight for a hunting camp filled with shifters. Hayden says the guy who came to his office is Paul Malone's brother."

"The guy from the hospital in Catamount?"

Jake nodded. "Hayden's says both of them are in deep with the smuggling group. He didn't want us to get trapped." Jake paused and shook his head. "It wasn't easy, but I backed off. I might be pissed, but I'm not stupid. Hayden thinks we need to peel off one of the leaders around here and see what kind of intel we can get. There are too many shifters involved here for it to be safe for us to try to go straight at them."

Phoebe fought the fear that rose inside at the possibility of Jake and Dane getting cornered by too many shifters. She abruptly sat on the bed, tugging the towel tighter around her. "Maybe we should go home. I didn't realize how big this thing was until we got out here. I don't want you and Dane to get hurt. I can't…" She paused to gather herself, fighting back tears.

Jake grasped her hands and knelt in front of her. "We're not going to get hurt. Did you miss the part where I backed off?"

She shook her head, taking another gulp of air. Before she'd let herself experience the full force of her feelings for Jake, it would have been terrifying to worry about his safety. Now, she could hardly bear the thought of something happening to him. He'd knocked through her well-honed defenses and taken residence in her heart. Though she'd been afraid for years of how to handle her feelings for him, the reality of being with him and allowing herself to hope went far beyond anything she could have imagined. He'd gone from being one of her dearest friends to literally holding her heart and body in his hands. Her body thrummed to life on its own accord when he was anywhere near her. Hope unfurled and shined light in the dark corners of her heart where she'd buried her feelings for him. She experienced a flash of intense anger toward Callen for exposing Catamount and its shifters.

Jake's thumb stroked across the back of her hand. He said her name softly. She met his eyes.

"It'll be okay. Dane and I talked on the way back. We were thinking we should head back to Catamount in a few days anyway. Maybe you and Shana should head back sooner?"

Anchored by his eyes, Phoebe shook her head. "I don't want to leave until you do."

He nodded. "Okay. Let's go get some dinner."

He started to stand, and she tightened her grip in his hands. "Promise me you'll keep me in the loop no matter what's happening."

He held her gaze. "I promise."

Chapter 13

Jake padded quietly through the trees. He and Dane were following Hayden into the foothills of the Gallatin range, one of the six mountain ranges surrounding Bozeman. They'd shifted once they made it out of sight. Hayden had shown them several caches of clothing and supplies hidden throughout the woods. Though mountain lions were prevalent out here, shifters still protected themselves by being prepared to shift into human form if needed. Hayden and Jake had done some online sleuthing last night and this morning and determined someone was using an abandoned hunting camp out here, one not known to be frequented by the smugglers. Hayden's suspicion was that Paul Malone was hiding out here. With Hayden's help, Jake had been able to identify many of the contacts he'd found, but who had been unnamed to Jake. Paul was one of them. Jake's prior investigative work had shown plenty of emails between Paul and others, but the trail had gone cold since Chloe's kidnapping.

They hoped to sneak up on Paul and overpower him. This, of course, hinged on their guess being accurate that he was the one out here using a satellite internet connection. Hayden led the way, moving with stealth through the trees. Dane wove through the trees at Jake's side, mirroring his pace. He and Dane had spent so many hours together in lion form that he could anticipate Dane's moves. They fought well in tandem, having grown up wrestling as boys and mountain lions. Though he'd grown to trust Hayden in the short time he'd known him, Jake hoped he could count on him if they had to fight. In all likelihood, Hayden had spent more time prowling in lion form than he and Dane had. Back East, they had to grapple with the extra layer of secrecy tied to the reality that mountain lions were considered extinct in the East.

For now, Jake flicked his tail and stretched, the cold air rippling through his fur. The snow grew deeper as they ascended into the foothills. Icy wind blew in gusts, catching the snow and swirling it in the air about them. Hayden paused and glanced over his shoulder. Jake and Dane walked to meet him, pausing on either side of him. Hayden swung his head to the side. The trees opened slightly in the distance and a small cabin sat nestled among them. Smoke drifted out of the stovepipe on the corner of the cabin. It was midafternoon with only a few hours of daylight left.

At Hayden's nod, they moved through the trees, winding around behind the cabin. They'd agreed Hayden would shift into human form and approach the cabin. Unlike Jake and Dane, he could fabricate a plausible reason for being out there. Working for Fish & Wildlife gave him a host of reasons to hike around the nearby areas. Jake and Dane would wait outside and be prepared to attack if needed. Once they were close enough and out of sight behind some boulders, Hayden shifted and immediately lifted a rock by one of the boulders, tugging out a bag of clothing. After dressing, he made his way to the cabin door, knocking only when Jake and Dane were positioned on opposite walls of the cabin.

Though Jake couldn't see, he recognized Paul's voice from the day he'd gone into the hospital. Paul greeted Hayden and then silence fell. There was a sudden roar, distinctly mountain lion. Jake dashed around the corner to find Hayden crouched, his tail flicking. Dane came out precisely when Jake did. Paul had shifted. He glanced among them, his golden eyes flicking from one to the other. Appearing to assess the reality of his chances in a fight, he snarled and bolted. Jake took chase with Dane and Hayden right behind him. Paul flew through the trees, weaving and dodging. Hayden pulled ahead and swiped at Paul, forcing him to dodge, breaking his pace. He fell into line in front of Jake.

Primal anger pulsed through Jake. His muscles bunched under him as he poised to leap. Flying through the air, he landed on Paul's back, sinking his claws in and throwing him down. Snow flew up around them. Jake didn't give an inch and held Paul down with his front paws. When Paul attempted to bite, Jake roared and sank his teeth into Paul's neck. The iron taste of blood seeped into his mouth. He held on until Paul went limp. Hayden and Dane stood on either side of them. Their breath bellowed into the air, mist curling around them. Paul was alive, but injured enough that he lay still.

***

Many hours later, Jake stood in the hotel bedroom while Phoebe glared at him.

"How come you didn't call as soon as you guys got to the police station?"

Jake took a slow breath. He was weary and tired after a long afternoon turned into an even longer evening.

After they'd made it back to Hayden's office, Paul's injuries had warranted a visit to the hospital. Jake found it ridiculous that the man who'd wasted time and space in the hospital in Catamount actually needed medical care now. Hayden had insisted they let him do the talking since he knew who was safe to talk with. Though it had chafed Jake, as well as Dane, they'd known it was the smarter move. After Paul was treated and released, they'd had a rendezvous at the local police station with a detective who was familiar with the smuggling activities of local shifters.

The upside was that Paul was talking. The downside was he was talking because he was scared. Jake had been startled to learn Paul believed Callen had been a leader in the smuggling network. That's why he'd headed to Catamount after Callen died and the kidnapping attempt on Chloe failed. Paul admitted he'd been unable to determine if anyone else in Catamount was involved beyond the lower levels of the network. He was skittish as hell because he'd survived three attacks in the woods by other shifters in the month before and after Callen's death. Paul knew he wasn't safe locally anymore, which was why he'd gone into hiding. Problem was he didn't know who was after him.

By the time they were done questioning Paul and left him with the local detective to be held on charges related to his smuggling activities, it was close to midnight. In the midst of all of it, Jake had only called Phoebe once when they made it back to town. She was none too pleased.

She stood before him, her dark eyes flashing and curls tumbling over her shoulders. Her gaze coasted over him. She reached out and fingered a tear in his shirt. He badly needed a shower. Though he'd come away from his encounter with Paul with little harm, he had several deep scratches where Paul had swiped at him, dried blood on his arms and torso, and a few healthy bruises.

"Phoebe, I left a message…"

She flung a hand up. "To say you'd made it back okay. That's it! We spent hours wondering when we'd hear something else. I just asked you yesterday to keep me in the loop, and you go and do this!"

She whirled away, her curls arcing in the air. The hotel room didn't leave much space, so she merely paced a few feet away from him. She stopped and looked out the window. Their hotel faced the foothills of one of the mountain ranges. A half moon rose above the mountains, the snow bright under its silvery glow. Stars sparkled in the cold, dark night. Phoebe hugged her arms tightly to her waist and sighed.

Jake stepped behind her and carefully rested his palms on her shoulders. When she didn't push away, he slid them down her arms and noticed she was shivering. He took a step closer and wrapped his arms around her. Her back pressed against his chest, and her lush bottom nestled into him. He couldn't help the lust that streaked through him. Ever since he'd let himself stop battling his feelings for her, he'd lost all control over his desire. All she had to do was *be*, and he was lost. He ignored his raging hard-on and held her close, nuzzling his head into the soft curve of her neck, that sweet spot where she stretched and almost purred every time he kissed her there. He held himself back as her body was taut with tension.

"You're cold," he murmured into her neck.

She nodded.

"I'm sorry I didn't call again."

Another nod.

"I'm not going to make excuses. Next time, I promise if I don't get you when I call, I'll call again."

Another nod, but this time he felt the tension ease slightly in her shoulders. He dared to drop a kiss on her neck. "Let's go home tomorrow."

She glanced over her shoulder and slanted her eyes in his direction. "Are you sure? Don't you guys want to look into a few more things?"

Jake lifted his head, still holding her close, and looked out over the mountains. "There's a lot more to tell you. It's fair to say, we've got some more work to do, but there's no sense in staying here for now. Hayden will keep tabs at this end. After we talked to Paul, we realized we needed to get back to Catamount and try to follow up on that end."

Phoebe rotated in his arms, so she was facing him. "Tell me everything." She paused, her eyes coasting over his face. "After you take a shower." A grin spread across her face as she placed her palm on his chest and firmly pushed him back. He wanted nothing to do with her being away from him, but when he reached to pull her back, she sidestepped and strode around him to the bathroom. Water started running, and she called his name. When she tore his clothes off, it wasn't for the reasons he hoped. She carefully looked him over and dusted kisses over his scratches before all but shoving him into the shower.

After a long shower, *by himself*, he came out to find Phoebe had left the bedroom altogether. She was in the shared area of the suite with Dane and Shana with a pizza on the table. Jake's hunger took over, and he gladly sat and devoured as much pizza as he could. When he sat back in his chair, Phoebe handed him a beer and draped her legs over his. He and Dane filled them in on the events of the afternoon. While they'd been busy with Paul, Phoebe and Shana had stayed in town and done their own sleuthing to discover that one of the known shifters in the area happened to have shifter cousins in Catamount.

"What?" Jake asked, swiveling his head between

Phoebe and Shana.

Dane's eyes widened, but he was too busy chewing to say anything.

Phoebe nodded. "Yup. We didn't meet the guy, but we were at a local café for lunch and when we mentioned where we were from, the woman waiting on us said her friend had family from Catamount."

Shana picked up at Phoebe's pause. "It's some guy named Carl Jasper. There's more than a few Jaspers in Catamount. The woman didn't know much beyond that, but she told us where he lived and we did a drive by."

Jake and Dane spoke in unison. "What?!"

Jake couldn't squash the fear that prickled under his skin. With Phoebe and Shana sitting right in front of him, he knew they were safe, but he was weary of unexpected events.

Shana rolled her eyes. "Oh God, don't you dare try to give us grief for driving by some guy's house when you were out chasing Paul through the woods."

When Jake turned to Phoebe, she merely arched a brow. He bit his lip, his breath coming out in a hiss.

Dane sighed. "Fine, we won't give you grief about it, but how about keeping us in the loop?"

Shana slanted her eyes at him. "Right. 'Cause you guys really kept us in the loop for hours this afternoon. You already knew we've been keeping our ears to the ground. We happened to stumble into a tidbit. All we did was drive by a house in the middle of the afternoon. I was hoping we'd get a glimpse of him. But it doesn't really matter because just knowing he has family in Catamount gives us a lead."

Phoebe tapped Jake with her foot. "You can do your magic online and see what connections we might find between Carl Jasper and any of the Jaspers in Catamount."

Jake knew it wasn't rational, but anger zipped through him. The idea of Phoebe being anywhere near anyone who might be a risk clamped a vice around his heart. He forced himself to take a slow breath and glanced over at her. Her dark eyes met his as she stroked her foot along his calf. He sighed and leaned back. He was bone tired. After a few more minutes of conversation, he heard Phoebe commenting that he needed to get to bed. He dragged his eyes open when she nudged him gently.

He fell asleep with her snug beside him, her head tucked against his chest. Moonlight fell across the bed, illuminating her features. Her long dark lashes left spiky shadows on her cheeks.

***

The following morning, they met with Hayden once more. Hayden had little to offer on Carl Jasper, other than to confirm he was a shifter and his social circles bumped into a few of the shifters known to be involved in smuggling. He wasn't flying high on the radar, which left more questions than answers. While they waited at the airport for their flight back to Maine, Jake started digging online to see what he could turn up about Carl Jasper and any of the Jaspers in Catamount. A quick search showed that Carl had flown back and forth between Montana and Maine several times a year for the past two years, most recently right after Callen died.

Jake closed his laptop when their flight was called, impatient to get back to Catamount, so they could see what else might turn up. As their plane ascended, he glanced over at Phoebe. He was beyond relieved that this time he wasn't chasing after her. He slipped his hand into her curls. She turned to him, her eyes holding a glimmer of worry.

"What?" he asked.

She shrugged. “It feels like we have more questions now.”

“Yes and no. We might have more questions, but we also have more directions to go.”

Her lips quirked in a rueful smile. “I suppose.” She lifted a hand and traced his mouth, her touch electric.

Chapter 14

Phoebe walked along the street in downtown Catamount. She'd just finished work at the hospital and needed to do some last minute Christmas shopping. Snow had fallen again last night, and the town green was blanketed with a heavy layer of snow. The wind had piled drifts in areas. The air was crisp and cold. She took a breath, savoring the hint of balsam and wood smoke. After taking care of her shopping, she pushed through the door into Roxanne's Country Store. Warmth enveloped her, along with the scent of holiday baking. The deli did a brisk business over the holidays, providing an array of goodies. She scanned through the busy deli as she stood in line, her eyes noting Noah Jasper at one of the tables.

Since they'd returned from Montana, Jake had been busy with his online sleuthing, and she found she was constantly searching out anyone in the extended Jasper family in Catamount. Though she knew the family, they weren't close, so she had to fight the urge to interrogate those she encountered. Jake had grudgingly acknowledged that he couldn't keep her out of the investigation and had only asked she return the favor she'd asked of him and keep him updated. She'd rolled her eyes at that and politely pointed out she'd already done so at every turn.

Noah Jasper had gone to high school with her and Shana. He'd been sought after by the girls in high school for two reasons—he was tall, dark and handsome, and he was reserved, which made him a challenge. Though Phoebe didn't know him too well, she'd always sensed he didn't quite enjoy the attention. In fact, it seemed to make him uncomfortable. He'd gone to college out of state, then off to the military, and only returned to Catamount in the last year or so. He was rumored to have been in the Special Forces in the military, but he kept such a low profile, Phoebe didn't know if that was the case or not. She did know that if he were, he would be formidable. A shifter and a specially trained military operative would be dangerous. She hoped like hell that he wasn't involved in the smuggling network.

Roxanne tilted her head and grinned when Phoebe stepped up to the counter. "What'll it be today?"

"Coffee and a lemon bar."

Roxanne quickly served her, her eyes speculative as she handed over the coffee. "What's this I hear about you and Jake?"

Phoebe had known the questions would start now that she and Jake were being open about their relationship, but it didn't stop the flush that spread across her cheeks. "What have you heard?"

"That you two finally came to your senses, and things are hot and heavy. To be specific, Gail Anderson, who apparently sees everything and anything, told me she saw you in a lip lock with him yesterday in the hospital parking lot." Roxanne's grin was wide and her eyes glinted with mischief.

Phoebe's flush made her face hot. She chewed her lip and sighed. "Gail's not making it up, if that's what you're wondering."

Roxanne put a hand on her hip. "No need to be embarrassed with me. I've been wondering how long you two would keep denying the obvious."

Phoebe's chest felt tight. Her thoughts tumbled out. "I wasn't trying to hide anything. I'm just kind of freaked out. I don't know where this is going, and I don't know what I'll do if it doesn't work out."

Roxanne's eyes softened. "Come here," she said, gesturing for Phoebe to follow her behind the counter.

Roxanne led the way through a swinging door into the kitchen and to the small office in the back. Before Phoebe had a chance to say anything, Roxanne swung around, hands on hips. "Don't go and get all tangled up in your head. Jake has loved you for years."

Phoebe sighed. "That's what he says, but how long did he swear up and down he'd never be with a woman who wasn't a shifter? I'm not…"

Roxanne cut in. "If he was going to insist on that, you wouldn't be with him now either. Plus, guys are idiots sometimes. He got all twisted up about a romance gone wrong and finally realized that what went wrong had nothing to do with whether or not she was a shifter. Let it go. I know you, and I know how you run in circles in your brain. You've got other things to worry about, so accept a good thing now that it pretty much slapped you in the face. I'm not even going to bother saying more about it. If you start getting worked up, call me so I can tell you to *stop*. Moving on, fill me in on what happened in Montana."

For a second, Phoebe was taken aback and found herself wanting to ask Roxanne more about how she knew Jake had loved her for years, but when she meet Roxanne's firm, knowing gaze, she elected to take her advice and stop worrying it to death for the moment. It had all seemed easier during those days in Montana when their time together felt like it was floating in a bubble, removed from their day to day lives. She wanted more than anything to surrender into what she had with Jake—it was bliss far beyond what she could have imagined. She took a breath and moved on, offering a summary of the events in Montana.

"Someone is related to the Jaspers…hmmm," Roxanne said. "Pretty much anyone that visits town crosses my radar one way or another. Let me think. Any ideas if he's been out here?"

Phoebe nodded. "Yup. Jake dug up his flight history, and he's been to Maine a few times a year the last two years. Jake's still searching to see what else he can find. The only Jasper I know a bit is Noah, and he's not exactly chatty."

Roxanne chuckled as she turned to leave the office, waving for Phoebe to follow her. "Not exactly, but he's here almost every day, so I've had more time than you to wear him down."

Phoebe watched Roxanne grab the coffee pot from behind the counter and begin winding her way through the tables, pausing to chat as she did. Noah glanced up with a smile when she stopped by his table.

***

Jake stood from his desk and stretched. He'd been at it all morning. Aside from his work on the investigation, he had a few jobs to take care of for companies he contracted with to manage their websites and provide tech support. The sun was low in the sky now, its rays filtering through the trees behind his office. A bright red cardinal was perched on a tree branch outside his window, a splash of color amidst the snowy landscape.

His office door opened and Dane stood in the doorway. “Come on, we’re meeting Hank over at Theo Jasper’s place.”

Jake stood and grabbed his jacket. He’d quickly discovered that Carl Jasper from Montana had routine online contact with Theo Jasper in Catamount. Though smuggling was never explicitly mentioned, vague references to business were. Jake had passed this on to Hank who reported that Theo was already facing legal trouble for tax evasion. As Jake rode beside Dane on the way out there, Dane offered a brief update.

“After you cued Hank onto Theo, he found out from the jail that Theo’s visited Randall a few times since his arrest. He wants to question him and see where it goes. He asked us to meet him there because Theo’s been known to make things difficult.”

Theo lived close to downtown Catamount down a quiet side street. When they arrived, Hank was already there. Jake and Dane met him by his car. Hank pushed away from the car and began walking to the house. “Let’s see what we get from him.”

Snow crunched under their boots as they walked up to the door. After they knocked, there was a rustling sound and then silence. The door flung open, and Theo stood before them. In a flash, he shifted and dashed away. Though Hank was a shifter, he shook his head sharply and gestured for them to follow. “He’s headed right for downtown. I don’t know what his game is, but I’ll be fielding calls left and right. I won’t be able to deflect talk if I’m running around in lion form. As for you two, do what you need to do.” Hank turned on his heel and climbed into his car.

Jake and Dane met eyes briefly. In silent agreement, they shifted. Jake's fur rippled over him. He bolted with Dane at his side. They dashed through the trees, cutting through yards and side streets. Theo wasn't too far ahead of them. He was also smaller and leaner in cat form, just as in human form. He was headed straight for the center of downtown. Adrenaline drove Jake to a fierce pace, Dane matching him step for step. When they saw the tip of Theo's tail as he dashed out of sight, they split up, circling to opposite sides. They came around the building to find Theo had paused. His head swung side to side. He appeared to be assessing his options. If he went forward, they'd end up at the town green.

Jake growled, his hackles rose. The only thing holding him back was the fact that they needed to run Theo out of the center of town. Theo leapt forward, racing down the street that led to the green. Jake and Dane gave chase. As they dashed behind Theo and burst into the open, Jake's eyes landed immediately on Phoebe who was walking down the street toward her car. Roxanne stood at the door of her store, her eyes wide at the sight of three mountain lions racing through town. Theo veered toward Phoebe. Primal fury surged through Jake as he leapt after Theo. He swiped at Theo right as Theo lunged for Phoebe.

Phoebe dodged out of the way, but Theo's claws caught her shoulder as she fell. Jake snarled and leapt for Theo's throat. Theo twisted out of the way and dashed to the side. Jake paused and glanced down at Phoebe. She shook her head sharply when he moved toward her. "Go," she hissed. "I'm fine." Relief washed through him, but it was brief. It was plain luck Phoebe hadn't been injured. Dane leapt past them. When Jake saw Roxanne heading toward Phoebe, he swung away. Rage pulsed through him as he raced behind Dane, swearing he'd make Theo pay for targeting Phoebe.

Theo weaved his way back toward his home. Dane caught him just as they leapt over the fence around his yard. Jake cleared the fence and found Dane grappling with Theo. Claws and fur were flying in swift succession. Dane backed off when he saw Jake. Jake knew Dane sensed he needed this fight. With a low roar, he pounced on Theo. Theo was smaller, but feisty and relentless. The fight dragged on with Jake sustaining several deep scratches. He kept Phoebe in mind and gritted through to dodge another swipe and drive Theo against the fence, pinning him to the ground. Theo snarled, but the fight was done. It took all of Jake's will not to sink his teeth into Theo's throat and tear it out. Only his human mind kept him in check. They had enough to deal with now that three mountain lions had been seen running through the streets of Catamount. A dead one would only add to the brushfire of rumors.

Theo eventually went limp. Jake bit into the back of Theo's neck and dragged him into the house, Dane right behind them. Only when Theo shifted back into human form did Jake and Dane follow. As soon as they did, Jake heard a female voice. Shana stepped into the kitchen where they'd entered the house.

"Hey boys, heard you might need some help." She held up their clothing and tossed it to them.

They waited with Theo until Hank arrived. Theo was sullen and silent. Hank entered the kitchen, his eyes landing on Theo immediately.

"Well, you decided to make as much trouble as you could. We were wondering if you were involved with the smugglers, and you confirmed it. All we did was show up and you pulled that stunt. If you think it's a smart move to draw attention to shifters, think again. You just put every single shifter everywhere at risk. Now what's it gonna be?

You gonna talk or not?"

"You can't hold me for anything."

"Sure I can. If you were hoping lots of people saw you, you picked a bad time. It's dusk and most everyone already went home from work. My guys have interviewed anyone downtown. Aside from Phoebe and Roxanne, we have only two other witnesses who aren't so sure what they saw. I'm happy to arrest you for assault against Phoebe because I know damn well you assaulted her. You won't be sharing a cell with either one of your buddies though."

Theo swore and glared at Hank. "What the hell brought you to my doorstep?"

Hank shrugged. "We know you have connections with the smuggling network in Montana. All we wanted to do was ask you about that. For all we knew, you didn't know a damn thing. But then you go and pull this bullshit."

Theo leaned back in his chair. Jake had to hold himself back. He wanted to pummel Theo's face in. His phone buzzed in his pocket. He tugged it out and saw Phoebe's number. He stepped outside. "Are you okay? I wanted to stay and make sure…"

Phoebe cut him off. "I told you I was fine. What the hell is going on, Jake? Why were you and Dane chasing that shifter through town? And who was it?"

Phoebe had seen him and Dane in lion form many times, so she'd be able to pick them out. As for Theo, most likely not.

"Theo Jasper. We met Hank at Theo's place to talk to him, and he took off. Are you sure you're okay? I'm leaving now. Dane and Hank's guys can handle the rest. Where are you?"

After Phoebe told him Roxanne had taken her home, Jake stepped inside to confer with Dane. Dane handed him his keys and assured him he'd pick his truck up at Phoebe's later.

Chapter 15

Phoebe tried to shoo Roxanne out of the house, but she wouldn't budge. Phoebe didn't take well to being fussed over and that's what Roxanne was doing.

"You can complain all you want. I'm not leaving until Jake gets here," Roxanne declared.

"But I'm fine! He knocked me over and barely scratched me. You're making too much out of this."

Roxanne slowly shook her head. "I can see you're fine, but if I leave you here alone, Jake will give me hell, so you're stuck with me."

Phoebe rolled her eyes and leaned back on the couch. Roxanne had helped her up after Theo had knocked her over and insisted on driving her home. Initially, she'd wanted to take her by the hospital, but she'd acquiesced when Phoebe pointed out that they didn't need any more attention drawn to the fact that three mountain lions had just bolted through the center of town. The only factor on their side was timing. Dusk had fallen, so the light was weak, and most businesses had closed up for the day already. Roxanne had called Rosie who'd zipped over from her shift at the hospital only to glare at Roxanne for wasting her time.

"Okay, I'm with you on freaking out about the fact that three mountain lions ran through town, but she's barely scratched. Maybe if she hadn't had her winter coat on, we'd have something to worry about. I have to get back to work, but call me later. I want the scoop," Rosie had said as she dashed back out the door.

Meanwhile, all Phoebe could think about was what was happening with Jake and Dane. She wanted to believe he and Dane would have no trouble cornering Theo, but for all she knew, there were others involved. She kept checking her phone and finally called him. He would be here any minute. As she turned to ask Roxanne if she wanted anything to eat, her front door flew open. Jake strode through the door and slammed it shut behind him. A gust of icy air flecked with snow swirled in with him as he took two long strides to stand in front of her. He fairly vibrated with potent energy. He started to reach for her and abruptly stopped, stuffing his hands in his pockets. His jacket hung open, his clothes were torn in a few places, and he bore his own scratches, including one that snaked down his neck under the collar of his shirt with dried blood smeared around it. Snowflakes were scattered in his hair and on his jacket. She moved to stand.

"No! You need to rest. Are you okay?" he asked quickly, his eyes coasting over her.

"I'm fine! All he did was knock me over. I barely even got a scratch…"

"Where?"

Phoebe deduced Jake wouldn't let her get a word in edgewise until she showed him how minimal her injuries were. She glanced at Roxanne who mouthed, "I told you so."

Phoebe pulled the collar of her blouse out of the way to reveal the sliver of skin Theo's claw had caught when he'd knocked her down. The scratch was bright red and only deep enough to be annoying. She figured it would itch like hell in a day or two.

Jake's breath hissed through his teeth and his shoulders settled. "He didn't hurt you when he knocked you over?"

Phoebe shrugged. "I'll probably have some bruising tomorrow, but nothing major." She stood, deciding enough was enough and shoved his shirt out of the way to see how far the scratch extended. "You're in much worse shape than me. What the hell happened?"

When she tugged at his shirt, the vicious red line wove its way out of sight. She turned to Roxanne. "Go get the first aid kit out of my bathroom." Turning back to Jake, she pushed his jacket off his shoulders. "Kitchen," she ordered.

Jake opened his mouth to protest, and she glared at him. "I need better light. Go." She gestured for him to walk ahead of her and followed him into the kitchen. Tugging a stool away from the counter, she pointed for him to sit. He started to protest, but appeared to think better of it when he saw the look in her eyes. He sat while Roxanne returned with her first aid kit. Phoebe pulled his shirt off to find he'd sustained multiple deep scratches on his chest and back. She fought to keep her emotions under control. This was Jake, the man she'd loved for as long as she could remember. The last few weeks had stitched her heart so close to his, she couldn't fathom a world without him. Seeing the evidence of the scuffle with Theo heightened her fear and worry about the events swirling around Catamount shifters. Callen had died for reasons they still didn't fully comprehend. Jake was in the middle of all of it, and she knew she couldn't stand it if something happened to him. Her throat tight and her heart beating painfully, she took a deep breath and marshaled her control.

With Roxanne quietly handing over items she requested, Phoebe quickly cleaned the scratches and bandaged them. Though a few were quite deep, they were just shy of needing stitches, not that Jake would have allowed it if she'd suggested he needed stitches. While she worked, he quickly filled her and Roxanne in on the rapid succession of events. Shana arrived mid-conversation. After the brief interruption for Shana to confirm Phoebe was okay, Jake continued.

"Honestly, all we did was show up to question him. He didn't have enough sense to keep his cool. I left before I learned anything new. Dane said he'd call with any updates." He caught Shana's eyes. "Anything happen after I left?"

Shana shook her head. "Hank decided it would be better to get him to the station for questioning."

Phoebe stepped away and leaned against the counter. "So what now?"

Jake shrugged. "Your guess is as good as mine."

Roxanne glanced between them. "This is bullshit. We've got to find out everyone local who's involved. I understand this smuggling network is way more than local, but we need to know who we can trust around here."

Jake nodded. "Agreed. I'm hoping maybe Theo has enough sense to talk. Otherwise, we'll all keep working on it."

Shana rested her hips on the table and shook her head sharply. "I was hoping we'd go to Montana and get this cleared up. All it did was give us more questions. Have you heard from Hayden since we got back?" she asked, directing her question to Jake.

Jake nodded. "A few emails, but nothing new. Hayden said from the start he didn't think the shifters involved in Bozeman were any different than Callen. They aren't running the show, they're just in it for the cash."

Phoebe swallowed the fear welling in her throat. Not only did she fear for Jake's safety, but also the safety of many other close friends and family. Roxanne glanced around the room. "I need to head back to the store. Come with me," she said, gesturing to Shana. "That'll be ground zero for rumors about who saw what tonight." She grabbed her jacket off a kitchen chair and shrugged into it. With a wave and a worried smile, she pecked Phoebe on the cheek and left with Shana right behind her.

Phoebe met Jake's eyes, so blue they took her breath away. He lounged on the kitchen stool. Leave it to him to manage to lounge in such a situation. His muscled chest and arms were scattered with scratches and bruises, now intermingled with a few bandages over the worst of them. He reached a hand out and hooked a finger over her jeans, tugging her to him. He instantly engulfed her in his arms and threaded his hand in his hair, holding her head close beside his.

She could feel the beat of his heart as she stood in the cradle of his protective embrace. He was quiet, but she could feel the tension vibrating through him. The tears she'd been holding back welled, one splashing through her lashes and landing on his shoulder. His breath drew in sharply and he pulled back incrementally, nudging her chin up with his knuckles.

"That scared the hell out of me," he whispered fiercely. "Now you're breaking my heart. I'm fine. You don't need to be worried."

She knuckled her tears away. "Yes I do! I just want this to stop. I want to find everyone who's involved here and run them out of town. I can deal with people halfway across the country being involved in this bullshit, but not right here. I don't want to see you end up dead like Callen!"

Jake closed his eyes for a moment, his shoulders rising and falling with a deep breath. "That's not gonna happen," he said firmly.

"You don't know that." She took a shaky breath, willing herself to calm down.

Jake tucked a wayward curl behind her ear, smoothing his hand over her hair. He met her gaze again. "I can promise you I'll do my damnedest to stay safe. I don't know how long it will take, but we'll figure this out."

Phoebe met his eyes and felt the ground give way beneath her. Emotions rushed through her in a wave. It was too much to finally allow her heart free rein to explore the feelings she'd buried for Jake, to experience the exhilaration of actually being skin to skin with him, and to fear for his life all at the same time. His eyes darkened. His lips crashed against hers, and she was lost. Sensation thundered through her, sweeping her in its wake.

Jake's touch was everywhere at once. His lips hot on her neck, the rough skin of his palms heightening the fervor inside of her. Clothes were scattered and the kitchen stool kicked over. Molten heat built in her center and spiraled outward. Sensation teemed within her as he lifted her roughly in his arms, resting her hips on the edge of the kitchen table. The spike of arousal arced higher with every touch. He tugged her roughly against him, his cock hot and hard against her core. He rocked his hips into her, claiming her lips in another searing kiss. She could hardly catch her breath. He pulled away, a sharp tug on her bottom lip with his teeth.

He murmured her name as he looked down between

them, dragging the head of his cock back and forth through her slick folds. Pressure gathered within. She teetered on the delicious edge of release, but he didn't allow her to topple over yet. When she gasped his name between ragged breaths, pleading for him to fill her, he finally did. He surged inside, sheathing himself fully inside the wet clench of her channel. Desire clawed within her, she was almost drunk with it. He held still for a long moment.

"Phoebe, look at me."

His voice was low and taut. She dragged her eyes to meet his. His gaze was hot, electric and tender at once. His forehead fell to hers and he began to move, slowly rotating in and out of her, driving her higher and higher. Quivers began to build inside of her until he grabbed her hips, his fingers digging into her skin, and growled her name. The gathering storm exploded, rushing over her, through her and around her. As she throbbed and clenched his heated length, he cried out, arching away from her before his head fell to her shoulder as he shuddered in her arms. After an indeterminate amount of time, awareness returned. She heard the soft crackle of the dying fire in the other room and the wind whipping through the trees outside.

Epilogue

Snow fell steadily, gusting in swirls with the wind. Christmas morning had dawned cold and misty, the air heavy with the scent of impending snow. Jake looked out the window of Phoebe's kitchen into the woods behind her house. The balsam boughs were heavy with snow. A stately oak, bare of leaves, stretched into the sky, its branches softly dusted with snow. A blue jay squawked and burst from the trees, landing on a bird feeder that hung in front of the kitchen window, its feathers a bright speck of color in the white background.

Phoebe walked into the kitchen, toweling her hair dry. Her dark curls hung around her shoulders. She was stunning. Not a speck of makeup on and her beauty shone through with her dark eyes sparkling, her lips bright and full, and her cheeks flushed. He pushed away from the counter and pulled her close for a kiss. She flushed deeper, a hint of uncertainty flickering in her eyes. Jake knew without a doubt that she loved him, but he sensed she retained a lingering disbelief that he felt the same.

He leaned away from her and rested his hips against

the counter, sliding his hands into the pockets of her jeans. “What do I have to do to get you to stop wondering if this is real?”

Her eyes widened, and her breath drew in sharply. She started to shake her head. He arched a brow. “Don’t act like you don’t know what I’m talking about. I suppose I have years to show you, but I might as well say it again. I’ve loved you for years. I was an idiot for way too long. I don’t want to be with anyone other than you. Ever. Before you start thinking it to death, just remember that I’m not going anywhere, so we have the rest of our lives for me to convince you. In the meantime…”

He slid one hand out of her pocket and into his, pulling out a small box. Phoebe’s eyes flew to his, damp with tears. He cleared his throat. “After this week, I decided I don’t want to wait for the right time. The right time is now. I can wait if you’re not ready to answer. This is my grandmother’s wedding ring. She gave it to me before she died and made me promise I wouldn’t even take it out until I knew who I was meant to be with.” He paused, his throat tight with emotion. “Then she said not to be stubborn about it. So that’s why I’m giving you this now. I wasted a lot of time being stubborn for reasons that don’t make much sense to me now. I’d love it if you were ready to wear this, but until then, you can keep it here.”

He’d thought this through over and over the last few days ever since he’d chased Theo through town. He thought he was ready for her to tell him she wanted to wait, but right here, right now…the thought terrified him. Phoebe was the single most important woman in his life, and he loved her completely. No one could ever hold the place she held inside in his heart. If she wasn’t ready, he would wait, but he’d rather not.

Her dark eyes met his, a tear rolling out of the

corner. He brushed it away with the back of his hand. She took a breath, her eyes softening. "It would be silly of me to act like I didn't already know my answer. I'm still getting used to…" She paused and gestured between them. "…us. But I've loved you for as long as I can remember." She carefully opened the small box and held still for a long moment. His grandmother's ring was platinum with a bright sapphire surrounded by tiny diamonds.

Phoebe looked up, her eyes bright with tears. She held her hand out for him to slide the ring on, her hand trembling softly. He laced his hands through hers and brought his lips to hers. They breathed in unison when he broke away.

"It's Christmas," she said softly. "We have to get going. I promised Roxanne I'd be there this morning to help cook."

Jake nodded. "I know. I'm ready whenever you are."

***

Phoebe glanced around at the room filled with friends and family. Catamount was home and contained all the people and shifters she loved the most. Though uncertainty reigned with the specter of recent events heavy, today was a day of celebration and community. Roxanne's Country Store was the central gathering place among the older Catamount shifter families and a few others. Her commercial kitchen made cooking much easier. The air was scented with hot cider, baked goods and ham.

Phoebe glanced down at her hand as she set a basket of fresh baked rolls on the table. Her heart stuttered at the sight of the beautiful ring Jake had given her this morning. She couldn't have made him wait if her life depended on it. He'd zeroed in on her lingering difficulty with accepting the joy that pervaded her heart, but it wasn't because she doubted him. It was simply so new, she needed time to adjust. After hours this morning of exclamations and the obvious joy their friends and family felt over their joining, she'd managed to forget, if only for a brief while, the fear and worry that had hung over Catamount since Callen had died and the lid on his secrets had blown off.

Jake stood across the room, conveniently standing in the archway leading into the back hallway where a small clutch of mistletoe hung. Phoebe threaded her way across the room, brushing her hands on her apron. When she reached his side, she didn't have to say a word. Jake lifted a hand, tucking a curl behind her ear, shivers chasing in the wake of his touch. His hand moved seamlessly down the side of her neck and around her shoulder, pulling her close for a kiss. It was mere seconds of sheer bliss, hot, searing and breath stealing. When he pulled away, his blue eyes met hers, possessive, tender and fiery at once.

Phoebe felt a nudge on her shoulder and glanced over to find Chloe grinning at her. "No hogging the mistletoe," she said.

Jake chuckled and moved out of the way, tugging Phoebe with him, his arm snug around her shoulders.

Hours later, they walked outside into the night. Holiday lights sparkled on the old lampposts lining the streets. Snow had fallen throughout the day and was finally slowing now. A fluffy, blanket of white coated the landscape, bright under the lights and the soft glow of the moon. Stars dotted the sky as they drove through the darkness. Though she knew there was much more to come until Catamount shifters were safe again, for tonight, the man who'd been her touchstone in more ways than one held her heart and body safe.

~The End~

Be sure to sign up for my newsletter! I promise - no spam! If you sign up, you'll get notices on new releases at discounted prices and information on upcoming books. Click here to sign up: http://jhcroix.com/page4/

Please enjoy the following excerpt from Fated Mate, the next book in the Catamount Lion Shifters Series!

(Excerpt from FATED MATE, CATAMOUNT LION SHIFTERS, BOOK 3 by J.H. Croix;)

Chapter 1

Liliana North watched the snow float down around her as she stood beside her car on the side of the road. It was an early winter morning in Catamount, Maine with snow barely falling as the clouds cleared. The sun was cresting the horizon, its rays bright against the wintery white landscape. The road wound through the outskirts of Catamount, a wooded tract of land on one side and a field on the other. The scent of balsam fir was sharp in the cold air. She leaned over to check her tire.

"Definitely flat," she said to herself. A crow squawked in reply. She glanced up to see the crow had landed on the roof of her car, watching her curiously. She glared at the crow who might be providing her some company, but would be of no help with her flat tire. She pulled her phone out of her pocket and sighed. Reception was notoriously spotty anywhere on the outskirts of Catamount. Catamount was situated in the foothills of the

Appalachian Mountains, the hills and valleys making merry with cell phone reception.

Liliana, Lily to those who knew and loved her, tugged her jacket tighter around her and looked down the road. It was just past seven in the morning, and she didn't expect too many drivers at this hour. Shaking her head, she set to work changing her tire. Moments later, she managed to send two of the tire lug nuts rolling on the icy surface and had to shimmy under her car to recapture them. She was on the ground, the snow cold against her back when she heard a car come to a stop and footsteps slowly make their way toward her.

"Need any help?"

The voice was low, gravelly, most definitely male… and sexy. *Seriously? How can you think a voice is sexy when you don't even know the man attached to it?* Lily rolled her eyes and brushed her hair out of her face. She knew the answer to her mind's taunting question. She was twenty-eight years old and somehow, despite her best efforts, she was still a virgin. Lately, she had sex on the brain. Between a few members of her inner circle falling in love lately and her own annoyance with her virginity, she couldn't seem to stop herself from assessing every man who crossed her path. *Yeah, but this is just some random guy who stopped to help you by the road.* She wished she had an off button for her tendency to converse with herself. She considered whether to tell the man with the sexy voice to carry on. She could use the help though because she wasn't so sure her spare tire was in good enough shape to use.

She stretched and curled her fingers around the last of the errant lug nuts. Holding them firmly in her grip, she wiggled her way out from under her car and almost choked when her eyes landed on Noah Jasper. Tall, dark, smoldering, enigmatic, and most definitely sexy as hell—that was Noah Jasper. Lily had many fantasies about Noah in high school. He'd been two years ahead of her and had half the girls in Catamount drooling over him. He stayed above the fray. To Lily's knowledge, he'd never dated anyone in Catamount. He'd gone straight to college and then on to the Marines. Rumor had it he'd been in the Special Forces. A few months ago, she heard Noah had moved back to Catamount.

There she was flat on her back in the snow and a flush raced through her at the mere sight of Noah. He leaned forward, stretching his hand out. She placed her hand in his and shivered at the contrasting warmth. Her hand was engulfed in his. Without appearing to exert effort, he steadily pulled her to her feet. Once she was standing, she tucked the lug nuts in her pocket, glanced up into his amber eyes and tried to keep from blushing. His mouth quirked slightly.

"What?" she asked.

Noah gestured to her hair. "You've got pine needles sticking out of your hair."

She reached up and felt several sticking straight up. She brushed her hands through her hair. When she tugged the last pine needle out, she glanced back at Noah who stood quietly. She gave her jacket a shake to knock the loose snow off. Of all the people to see her with pine needles in her hair and snow covering her back, Noah was most definitely not her choice. He was a sexy and mysterious shifter who'd moved away, while she was a boring, quiet computer programmer. In the world they lived, she was the least likely to be noticed. Catamount, Maine was a town filled with mountain lion shifters. While Lily came from one of the oldest shifter families in town, she tended not to attract attention and preferred to keep it that way. Noah, on the other hand, attracted plenty though he didn't seem inclined to care.

She forced her attention to the moment. "Thanks for stopping. I got a flat tire, but I'm not so sure my spare's in good enough shape."

Noah met her eyes again and nodded. Damn, he was handsome. He had chiseled features. As with most shifters, his face had a feline cast, his cheekbones angling up, eyes tilting at the corners. His almost black hair made his amber eyes stand out. His mouth was sensual and full. He nodded to her spare tire. "Mind if I take a look?"

Her heart pounded so loudly, she could barely think. She nodded quickly. "Go ahead."

Noah rolled the tire away from where she'd leaned it by her car and ran his eyes over it, giving it a push. The rubber gave easily under the pressure of his hand. He looked up and shook his head. "It needs air." He lifted it and strode to the back of his truck, tucking it under the cap. Without a word, he quickly adjusted the jack and lowered her car.

"What are you doing?"

Noah swung her way, his amber eyes sending her belly into a tailspin of flutters. "Making sure your car's safe for now. We can't leave it jacked up like that. I'll drop you off wherever you need to go and stop by here later after I get your tire repaired."

"Oh, um, you don't need to do all that." Lily felt off-kilter and confused to have him so quickly step in to help.

Noah met her eyes again. She didn't know how she could handle riding in a car with him. His proximity had all but turned her to mush. Wet heat coiled through her when he arched a brow. "I'm not going to leave you here, and it's not safe for you to try to drive on that spare." He glanced at his phone. “Since there’s no phone reception here, you can’t think I’m going to drive off. What’s your plan, wait for the next person to come along?” Suddenly, his eyes widened and then a look of bitterness followed. “Ah, I get it. You think I had something to do with the mess my uncle landed in?”

Lily shook her head forcefully. “No! I wasn’t even thinking about that.” As she spoke, she considered that if she hadn’t been so bowled over by him, she probably would have wondered. The last few months in Catamount had been marked by turmoil and betrayal after the death of a shifter unraveled the secrets he left behind. Callen Peyton had died in mountain lion form when he was killed by a car in Connecticut, of all places. Lily’s brother, Jake, was the one who uncovered Callen’s plans to sell the services of Catamount shifters to a drug smuggling network out West. The ensuing events had involved a kidnapping and a cross-country trek to Montana.

Noah’s uncle, Theo Jasper, had been arrested a few weeks ago for his involvement in the smuggling network. That was the public story. The full story circulated only among the mountain lion shifters in Catamount. The glaring detail missing for everyone else was that Theo had shifted into mountain lion form and taken Lily’s brother, Jake, and another friend on a wild chase through town first. This little event was yet another in a cascade of events in Catamount that had driven deep fissures in the shifter community in Catamount.

Catamount shifters had stayed safe for centuries by keeping their existence a well-guarded secret. Callen’s death and the tentacles of the drug smuggling network threatened to blow that secrecy to pieces. Lily considered that Noah had a point. Though she hadn’t been thinking of it right now, she figured he’d had many eyes cast in doubt on him since Theo was arrested. She was so twisted inside at being near him, her tendency toward suspicion had been turned off. She took a breath and met his eyes.

"I really wasn't thinking about that, Noah. I'm not so great at accepting help, that's all." Her words were true, but the other truth was it was hard to know who to trust in Catamount anymore. Even though Noah sent her body into a tizzy, her gut told her he was trustworthy. Her breath misted the air. The crow that had been sitting on her car earlier squawked from a nearby tree. Snow sparkled where the sun's rays landed.

"I'm guessing it's not so fun being you these days in Catamount," she finally said.

Noah shrugged, his eyes guarded. "Theo's an ass. I barely know him. He's my dad's brother, and I wasn't exactly close to my dad before he passed away. I get why people would wonder, but trust me, I had nothing to do with any of that bullshit. My mom's about half out of her mind about it, but I figure we have to wait until the dust settles." His words were matter-of-fact and polite. He met her eyes again. With the barest nod, he continued. "Did you want that ride after all?"

Lily nodded, hugging her arms around her waist, shivering when a gust of wind blew across the road, stirring snow in a swirl. "Let me get my purse." She rushed over to her car and grabbed her purse. Noah waited by his truck. When she reached his side, he opened the door for her. She hadn't realized how cold she'd gotten until he closed the door and the warmth of his truck cab seeped through her.

When he climbed inside, he sat still for a moment before turning to her. "If I came across like a jerk, I didn't mean to. This whole…" He paused and gestured vaguely. "…mess makes me sick."

"You didn't come across like a jerk. Everyone's on

edge these days." She didn't add that he set her on edge in an entirely different way.

He held her eyes for a long moment, and she felt the flush crawling up her neck and face. He was way too sexy for her to think straight. Her traitorous body swirled with heat. Noah was seriously out of her league. There was a reason she was still a virgin and it definitely wasn't because she was saving herself for anything. It was because she wasn't the kind of woman men noticed. Female shifters were supposed to be sexy, but even though she couldn't quite say what she was lacking, she knew Noah had only noticed her because her car was broken down.

He nodded slowly. "On edge is one way to put it." He turned away and put his truck in gear. "Where to?"

***

Noah glanced over at Lily and took a breath. Lily North was about the cutest woman he'd ever laid eyes on, and he couldn't figure out how he'd never noticed her before. Her golden brown hair fell in loose waves around her shoulders. She'd tried to tidy her hair after she pulled the pine needles out, but had only slightly succeeded, which was just fine with him since it only made her even cuter. Her blue eyes darted sideways to meet his, and she bit her lip. He forced himself to take another breath. Damn. He'd known Lily for as long as he could remember, but only in passing. It wasn't that he didn't notice her, but he'd never gotten close enough to her to realize she was flat out gorgeous with her sky blue eyes, her flushed cheeks and her petite curvy body.

They were both from shifter families in Catamount. Difference was, Lily's family was revered in Catamount while his family, on the other hand, was probably better forgotten. Theo's involvement in the drug smuggling scandal was just another notch in their list of misdeeds. Noah's father, Willis Jasper, had died from a heart attack five years ago. Noah had felt only relief and regret at his death. Willis had been abusive to his mother for as long as Noah could remember. Just as with humans, there were plenty of shifters who wanted nothing more than easy power. Knocking around anyone close was Willis's way of finding power. Noah had cultivated the skill to stay out of the way. The only thing he could thank his father for was his skill at staying quiet and almost invisible, which had served him well in the Marines and enabled him to climb his way into the Special Forces. Stealth missions came easily to him.

Noah moved back to Catamount a few months ago when he found out his mother's health was failing. She'd said nothing to him about it, but his aunt had called him and told him his mother had been diagnosed with lung cancer. Since he'd come home, he'd learned from her doctor that her cancer was Stage Three and had spread to her spine. Sadly, she'd never smoked in her life. The doctor had explained that she was likely exposed to radon gas for years. New England had high rates of radon present. Many homes dealt with this by installing systems to filter it out, but their home had never had one.

His mind flashed to this morning when he found her coughing up blood in the kitchen. He immediately shoved the memory away. She was sick and most likely dying. He had to find a way to come to terms with that. In the narrow world of his childhood, his mother had been the only bright spot in his heart. Though she'd never managed to walk away from Willis, she'd done what she could to shield Noah and been a source of steady support and love for his entire life.

He hadn't thought twice about moving back to

Catamount when he heard she was sick. While his career in the Marines had saved him in many ways, he'd been moved to administrative duties on base after sustaining multiple injuries in a bombing in Afghanistan. While he could have bided his time and been cleared for full duty again, he couldn't even consider leaving his mother to die alone. His father may have been a big part of the reason he left Catamount, but his mother was what kept his heart tethered.

He'd also missed Catamount—the stark seasons, the weathered beauty of the forests here, the nooks and crannies hiding in the Appalachian Mountains, and being in the one and only place he felt safe being true to himself as a shifter. While he'd lived away for over a decade, he could count on one hand the number of times he'd shifted into mountain lion form while he was away. It wasn't safe, so he barred the door to that part of himself. It wasn't like shifters walked freely around as mountain lions in Catamount, but at least half the town were shifters, and the expansive wilderness nearby allowed shifters to roam freely when they wanted. In the few months he'd been home, he'd spent hours and hours roaming the forest and foothills—feeling and flexing into his mountain lion again.

Lily's phone jangled—a cherry chirp of a ring—and she jumped in her seat. Noah canted his eyes sideways to find her fumbling for her phone in her purse. As soon as she got it out, she dropped it. The phone slid out of sight under the seat. He bit back the urge to laugh. She looked so flustered and damn cute.

"Dammit!" She leaned forward, but quickly sat up again. "No way I can reach it. I can't even see it." She sighed and leaned back.

"I'll get it for you when we stop," he offered.

He looked over at her when he stopped at an

intersection near downtown Catamount. She was looking out the window, chewing her lip and twirling a lock of silky hair around her finger.

"Where should I drop you off?"

She turned to him. When her gorgeous blue eyes collided with his, she flushed, uncertainty flashing in the depths of blue. She bit her lip, and a jolt of lust hit him. Noah didn't know what had come over him, but his body had all kinds of things to say about Lily. He couldn't remember the last time he'd even noticed a woman. He'd done his share of dating, but nothing ever went beyond light and easy. After the nightmare of watching the devastation his father wrought on his mother, he didn't believe in the fairy tale of love and romance. Hence, he threw himself into his career and kept relationships superficial. The effect Lily was having on him was—unusual. He wanted to know what lay behind those flickers of uncertainty. His body wanted to tug the bundle of her—lush curves and softness—into his lap and kiss her senseless.

He shackled his urges and focused on the moment. "You can drop me off at my brother's office," she finally said.

The light changed and he drove through the intersection, turning toward the center of downtown where Jake's office was. "You work with Jake?"

She shook her head. "Not really. Sometimes I help him with projects."

"I know Jake's does something with computers, but what do you do?"

"Jake does coding, website building and is what most people call a forensic computer expert. Short description: he can hack like nobody's business, but he keeps it legal. I work in the same field, but we do different things. I work the other side of hacking by identifying network vulnerabilities and helping create fixes. I freelance and mostly work from home. When Jake needs extra help on something, he usually calls me."

"Damn. Guess you could say being brilliant runs in the family, huh?"

Noah pulled up in front of Jake's office as he said this. He turned to Lily. Her cheeks were flushed again. She shrugged, still twirling that lock of hair around her finger. "Not really. We both like computers though." She glanced toward Jake's office and back to Noah. "So, um, do you want me to see if Jake can deal with the tire?"

Noah couldn't explain it, but there was no way he was giving up the chance to see her again. Even if seeing her only meant picking her up with the repaired tire and returning her to her car. "Nah. I got it. How long were you planning on being in town today?"

"I hadn't really planned much. What time were you thinking of heading back out?"

"I have a few errands to run, but I should be done this afternoon. How about I pick you up around two?" He left out that what he would be doing for most of the day was sitting with his mother while she got her latest round of chemotherapy.

Lily nodded. "Sure. That'll work." She moved to get out of the car. "Oh, I have to get my phone!"

She climbed out and looked under the seat. Noah watched her for a moment and leaned down to see if he could find her phone. Just as his hand closed over it, all the way over to the driver's side, he looked up to say something and found Lily's face inches from his.

Her blue eyes widened when he met her gaze. The flush simmering under the surface of her skin flared on her cheeks. Her lips, plump and an almost perfect bow shape, were so tempting, his breath hitched and pulse pounded. His eyes, clearly under their own control, flicked down. She wore a scoop neck shirt, which hung forward since she had leaned over. The generous curves of her breasts were on display, a glimpse of blue lace teased him. *Holy hell.* Her ivory skin was taut. He could see the beat of her pulse in her neck.

She froze and suddenly scrambled away. His body literally ached for a split second. He'd come so close to touching her, the loss of the chance was a sharp pang. He forced himself to take a breath before he sat up. He held his palm out, her phone on it. "Here you go. So, uh, I'll see you this afternoon?"

Lily brushed her hair back, tucking those honeyed locks behind her ears, and pulled her jacket together in front, hiding her delectable breasts from his view. He doubted she had a clue the effect she had on him. It was like a lightning bolt out of nowhere. He was beyond relieved he was sitting down with his jacket covering the bulge in his pants. She nodded quickly and snagged her purse. She turned to leave when he realized she hadn't taken her phone from him.

"Hey, did you want your phone?"

She whirled back. "Oh! Yes, yes, of course." She reached out, her fingers brushing his when she took the phone. "See you in a little bit. Thanks for the ride." She turned away quickly and all but ran up the walkway to her brother's office.

Available now!

Fated Mate **(Catamount Lion Shifters, Book 3)**

Chosen Mate (Catamount Lion Shifters, Book Two)

Go here to sign up for information on new releases: http://jhcroix.com/page4/

Thank you for reading Chosen Mate (Catamount Lion Shifters)! I hope you enjoyed the story. If so, you can help other readers find my books in a variety of ways.

1) Write a review!
2) Sign up for my newsletter, so you can receive information about upcoming new releases at http://jhcroix.com/page4/
3) Follow me on Twitter at https://twitter.com/JHCroix
4) Like my Facebook page at https://www.facebook.com/jhcroix
5) Like and follow my Amazon Author page at https://amazon.com/author/jhcroix

***

Catamount Lion Shifters

Protected Mate

Chosen Mate

Fated Mate

Destined Mate

Diamond Creek Alaska Novels

When Love Comes

Follow Love

Love Unbroken

Love Untamed

Tumble Into Love

Last Frontier Lodge Novels

Chosen Mate (Catamount Lion Shifters, Book Two)

Christmas on the Last Frontier

Love at Last

Acknowledgements

To my husband for cheering on my writing every step of the way, especially when I'm tapping away on my keyboard. Gracious thanks to Laura Kingsley who holds me to a high standard with her editing and makes my writing better every time. Clarise Tan at CT Cover Creations weaves magic with my covers. A standing ovation to my readers—thank you, thank you, thank you!

Author Biography

Bestselling author J. H. Croix lives in a small town in the historical farmlands of Maine with her husband and two spoiled dogs. Croix writes sexy contemporary romance and steamy paranormal romance with strong independent women and rugged alpha men who aren't afraid to show some emotion. Her love for quirky small-towns and the characters that inhabit them shines through in her writing. Take a walk on the wild side of romance with her bestselling novels!

CPSIA information can be obtained
at www.ICGtesting.com
Printed in the USA
LVOW10s1523091217
559232LV00030B/1012/P

9 781530 006427